THE SERGEANT'S TALE

by

Melvin Ward

ISBN 9781696744331

Cover Design by the author

Chapter I

The air was thick with smoke and the smell of burning. It should have been a pleasant June morning judging by the days that had gone before, but you couldn't tell whether it was or not. The smoke hung heavily over everything, obscuring the sun - if there was any sun - clogging the throat, scouring the mouth and depositing a thick layer of grime on skin and clothes. Alfie Holland hawked and tried to spit onto the rubble, but he couldn't summon up enough liquid to do it properly. Wearily, he clambered down the heap of bricks and roof tiles that had once been a house until he reached the road, then he turned and looked up and down the street. It was a very ordinary, respectable sort of street, an orderly row of houses each standing in its own little garden - but now, in the middle of it like a broken tooth in an otherwise neat and perfect mouth, there was that pile of rubble.

He turned away and sat down in the road. Number thirteen, he thought. Unlucky for some. Number eleven Botolph Street was intact, immaculately neat. Number fifteen had a couple of windows blown out but other than that stood as normal. Number thirteen no longer existed.

The funny thing was, there was nobody about. Botolph Street was deserted. The neighbours had all been there shortly after the all clear sounded, when the Civil Defence rescue team arrived. They meant well, poking about in the ruins, trying to help but basically just getting in the way, not knowing what they were doing, a danger to themselves and everybody else. After rescuers had found the bodies carried them away, the locals had quietly dispersed, wandering off back to their homes. Now there was nobody in sight, nobody rushing out to offer tea and comfort. It just wasn't that sort of area. Pity, he thought. He could have done with a cup of tea, or even better a glass of beer. Anything to wash the sour taste of smoke and brick dust out of his mouth.

Alfie sat down on the curb, deliberately turning his back on what was left of number thirteen and taking off his ARP helmet to lay it on the ground. It left an uncomfortable line of sweat and grime around his forehead and he was better off without it now the bombs had stopped falling. He opened his gas mask bag and pulled out of it a package, more or less square and wrapped in greaseproof paper. Folding the paper back, he picked up a thick sandwich and looked at it appreciatively for a few seconds before taking a large bite.

"You're supposed to keep a gas mask in there, Alfie, not your sandwiches."

The voice came from behind him, quite close, and Alfie looked round, startled. A police constable in full uniform was approaching, pushing a bicycle. He was a big man, heavily built with a conspicuous paunch stretching his tunic, and he looked too old to be a serving policeman; the small amount of hair that was visible beneath the helmet was grey. The uniform, like everything else on that day, was coated with dust.

"Oh it's you, Jack. You took me by surprise. I didn't think there was anybody about. Where did you pop up from?"

The policeman stopped beside him and nodded back in the direction he'd come from. "Side road. Anyway, what about that gas mask? A man in your position should be setting an example."

"Look here, a gas mask wouldn't have done me any good, would it? I mean, there hasn't been any gas, has there? A sandwich, on the other hand, can be a real life saver." He took another large bite from the sandwich as if to prove his point. "I've been up all night, I was already on duty when all this started and I'm getting a bit long in the tooth for keeping those sort of hours. Still, I dare say I'll get back to the centre when I've finished my breakfast. They'll manage without me until then."

"I suppose they will. There's firemen and rescuers from all over the county there. It's a real mess, though."

"I know. The High Street was burning when I left."

"A lot of it still is. And St George's has gone."

"Gone? What, the church?"

"The whole bloody street. As a matter of fact, the church tower's about the only thing still standing. There's broken glass everywhere." He stared down at the flat tyres of his bicycle disconsolately. "That's why I'm pushing this thing instead of pedalling it."

"How about the cathedral?"

Jack shrugged. "Can't say for sure. You can't see anything in all this murk. Last I heard it was basically all right - just a some bits chipped off the corners, as it were. I'm told there was a few incendiaries landed on the roof, but the Fire Watch managed to chuck them off before they did much damage."

"That's something, anyway."

"I suppose so."

The two of them lapsed into a brief silence. The constable turned and surveyed the ruin of number thirteen. "How are Mr and Mrs Berwick?"

"Are they the couple who lived here?"

"That's right."

Alfie took another bite of sandwich. "Dead," he said indistinctly through a mouthful of bread and cheese. "We got the bodies out."

"Out of the house? What did they think they were

doing in the house through all that? They've got an Anderson shelter in the back garden."

"I know, I saw it. And I thought the same as you. But the silly beggars were still in the house, no doubt about it - in fact, it looked as if they'd been still in bed when the bomb hit. I can't believe they slept through it, even if they'd both been deaf as posts the vibrations would have woken them. So what they thought they were doing, God alone knows."

"Yes, it was a hell of a racket while it lasted, wasn't it?"

"It was. Reminded me of the artillery barrages in the last war, and that's something I don't like being reminded of." He stuffed the last of the sandwich into his mouth and pushed the greaseproof wrapper back into his gas mask bag. "Oh well, no rest for the wicked. I'd better get back and see if I can make myself useful." He stood up and the two of them gazed at the remains of number thirteen. "Silly beggars," Alfie repeated his earlier judgement. "Not much of an epitaph, is it?"

Jack ignored the comment and pointed up the uneven slope of rubble. "What's that dog doing up there? The Berwicks never had a dog, not that I know of."

"How should I know? It's just a dog, probably a stray, sniffing around the way they all do. Scruffy looking animal, isn't it?"

It was. The dog was a mongrel of some sort, mostly lurcher by the look of it, thin with matted fur, and it had been prowling amongst the wreckage of the house. Now, however, it had settled in one spot. It stood with its head on one side, staring down. Then, suddenly, it started digging frantically, front paws scratching feverishly at the bricks.

"It can smell something there," said Jack.

"Probably the remains of last night's dinner. I expect

it's hungry. I know how that feels."

Jack shook his head slowly, doubtfully. "Could be, I suppose, but I don't think so. Look at it, it's going mad at that one spot. It'll tear its paws ragged if it goes on like that."

Alfie shrugged. "Leave the beast to it. I've got other things to do."

"I don't know... Look here, no offence intended but you did search for anyone else in the wreckage, didn't you?"

"Course we did!" Alfie was indignant. "What do you think we are? We've done this before, you know. Obviously we can't go through every square inch, but we had a good poke around. Besides, the neighbours said there'd be nobody else there, only the Berwick couple. Sure of it, they were. Nobody else lived there."

"That's true enough, but they could have had visitors or something."

"At that time of night? And with them in bed? It's not likely, is it?"

"Not likely, no," Jack admitted. "Still... Look, as a favour to me, hang around for a few minutes while I go and take a glance at what that dog's getting so worked up about."

"If you like. Watch yourself on that rubble though. It's none too safe and you're no lightweight, are you?"

The policeman didn't answer, but started over the ruin. Above him, the dog stopped its scrabbling and stood watching him, ears pricked up and tongue hanging out of a panting mouth. As he drew closer, treading carefully as his big feet in their heavy boots dislodged fragments of brick and sent them clattering down the slope, the dog turned and ran away. Alfie shook his head at such an exhibition of folly, sat down again and lit a cigarette. Let him get on with it. Jack reached the spot where the dog

5

had been digging and stood looking down. After a while he took off his helmet, scratched his head then replaced the helmet. Alfie suppressed a laugh. Jack leaned forward - he looked very precarious up there - and threw a few bricks to one side. Then he bent down and heaved up one end of a wooden beam that looked like a roof timber, maybe a rafter.

"Here," Alfie shouted, "I told you to be careful, didn't I?"

Jack ignored him, lifted the end of the rafter and shoved it over to one side. There was the ominous sound of falling bricks and a cloud of dust rose into the air. Jack put a hand over his face until it had settled, then leaned forward again, looking down. Slowly he straightened up, turned and started to make his way back to the pavement. When he got there he stopped to brush some of the dust from his uniform.

"Well Alfie, I'm sorry to tell you but you did miss one after all."

"There's another body?"

"There is. It's down quite deep though, looks as if it might have been in the cellar. And I'll tell you something else..." He paused for dramatic effect. "I couldn't see properly because I hadn't got my torch with me, but I'm pretty sure it didn't get there last night. It's been dead longer than that. A lot longer. I shall have to report this, Alfie. Can you hang about here for a bit while I get back to the station? Just to keep an eye on things?"

"Yes, if you like. But..."

"I'll leave the bike here, I'll be quicker without it. I'm sure it'll be safe in the capable hands of the Civil Defence. That's you, that is, in case you were wondering." He started off without another word, walking quickly down the street. Alfie stared after him, opened his mouth to shout something, some question, but couldn't think what to shout. After the heavy figure of the constable had disappeared into the haze of smoke, he dropped his cigarette and squashed it with the toe of his boot. Well, he couldn't just leave it at that, could he? The curiosity was too much, he had to take a look. Besides, unlike the policeman he had his torch with him.

He clambered carefully back up the heap that had been number thirteen, more practised and sure-footed than Jack had been; lighter too, less likely to disturb anything underfoot. When got to where Jack and the dog before him had been, he could immediately see the hole in the rubble that Jack had created by shifting the rafter. It was a deep hole, going beneath where the floorboards had been. He stood over it, peering down, feet set apart to steady himself. There was something there, right enough. Something that looked as if it might be a body.

Down in the back garden, the dog was still there. It sat on the roof of the Anderson shelter, staring up at him. There was something disconcerting about that mute stare, almost as if the dog knew exactly what he was doing.

Alfie took out his torch, directed it down into the hole and switched it on. At first the beam wavered around but after a few seconds he got it steady. It caught some white object and Alfie found himself looking down at what was unmistakably a human skull. He quickly switched off the torch and straightened up.

Down in the garden, the dog barked once, sharp and loud, then turned and ran off.

Chapter II

The train was only four minutes late, which wasn't bad considering the problems of wartime transport. It pulled into Canterbury West station at precisely twenty four minutes past ten in the morning. Eileen Chambers was sure of that, because she checked her watch as the engine drew to a halt. It was a reliable watch, a watch that always kept good time. With a sense of relief she pulled her kit bag from the rack and stepped down from the carriage onto the platform. The journey may have been punctual but it hadn't been very pleasant.

The train had been crowded, as so many of them were, and she had been able to find only one compartment with an empty seat. She'd had to share the compartment with an elderly woman who possessed a piercing voice and hadn't stopped talking for the entire duration of the journey, even though nobody was listening to her. Even worse, there had been two young merchant seamen who had been competing with one another to win her attention the whole time. The WAAF uniform and the sergeant's stripes hadn't seemed to put them off at all - the opposite, if anything. And worst of all, it had been a No Smoking compartment. The first thing she did on the platform was to put down her bag and light a cigarette.

"I'll carry that for you, if you like." One of the merchant seamen, persistent to the last, had appeared at her elbow and was reaching for the cylindrical duffel bag that held her kit. She snatched it up quickly.

"There's no need, thank you. It's not heavy. Besides, it's my kit and you always carry your own kit."

"Oh well, please yourself." He finally gave up and walked away down the platform. Eileen followed more slowly, making sure the distance between them increased before they left the station. Even then she paused for a couple of minutes in the grandiose but rather bleak portico that formed the entrance and exit, finishing her cigarette while the crowd dispersed. She was going to be early for her appointment anyway, it wasn't until eleven o'clock and there wasn't far to go. Finally, she stubbed out the cigarette, slung the kit bag over her shoulder and started to stroll in a leisurely way along the now almost empty Station Road West. It made a change to walk so slowly; there was an instinctive urge after all her training to stride out or even march, but she forced herself to keep to the unhurried pace.

She turned left at the end of the road into St Dunstan's. There was some damage to the old buildings there, but not as much as she'd imagined from the newspaper reports. They always exaggerated, of course, one expected that. She walked along St Dunstan's towards the grey stone bulk of the Westgate, the old entrance to the city. The road ran through the gate where it became St Peter's then the High Street and as she approached she could see through it to the streets beyond. What she saw came as something of a shock, despite what she had heard and read. The newspapers hadn't exaggerated after all. It was a scene of utter destruction. One side of the street was in ruins. Even now there were still people, many of them in uniform but some not, clearing rubble - and this was some three days after the main raid. A faint smell of burning persisted in the air and caught at the throat. The air was still, of course, on such a traditional June day, so there had been no wind to disperse it. Eileen stared for a few minutes, fascinated despite herself to witness such a scene. Then, resolutely, she turned and walked through the covered pedestrian passageway to the left of the stone towers. At the end of it she couldn't resist one more lingering look at the devastation before turning into Pound Lane.

The police station was only a few yards along the lane and she stopped outside it to consult her watch: she was early, as predicted. Well, it was always better to be early than late. The building towered above her, solid brickwork topped by pointless but symbolic crenellations. It wasn't particularly big, really, only two storeys in fact - but the crenellations made it look taller than it was. It had a rather forbidding look which was probably appropriate for its purpose; very stern and flat, with windows recessed into pointed gothic arches edged by grey stone quoins. She mounted the steps to the entrance, feeling rather as if she were voluntarily going into a prison. Or a pound, come to think of it; for some reason, that connection of names had never occurred to her before.

Inside, the building was disappointingly prosaic and official. It could have been any public building anywhere in the country, with its patriotic posters promoting the war effort and its closely typed notices pinned to boards on the walls. The desk was manned - if that was the right word under the circumstances - by an extremely thin youth with an anaemic complexion marred by virulent acne. His uniform was far too big for him, hanging loosely on his emaciated frame. Eileen noticed the WRC on the epaulettes; a war reserve constable. It looked, she thought to herself, as if they were scraping the bottom of the barrel. A more obvious failure of the military recruitment medical examination she had never seen. She approached the counter and dropped her kit bag to the floor.

"Can I help you, miss?" The voice was a boy's, not a man's. If he'd been in a choir he'd probably still be singing treble.

"I have an appointment with Inspector Jeffrey at eleven. I'm early I know, so if he isn't ready, I'll wait."

"Let me see..." He consulted a book that lay on the desk in front of him. "Oh yes, I see. You must be Miss Chambers, is that right?" Eileen shook her head patiently and pointed without speaking to the stripes on her arm. The youth looked baffled for a moment before understanding dawned. "Oh. Oh yes, of course. *Sergeant* Chambers."

"That's right."

"No offence intended, sergeant. If you'll kindly wait here for a moment I'll go and have a word with the inspector and see whether he's free."

"You do that, constable." Eileen stood where she was and looked aimlessly around the room. The youth disappeared quickly through a door behind the counter, leaving her alone. No one else appeared to need the services of the Kent constabulary on that day.

Beyond the door, the WRC hurried along a short corridor and knocked hesitantly on a closed door. A voice called out "Enter" and he pushed the door open. Inside was a small plain office equipped with the usual desk, filing cabinets and shelves. Behind the desk Inspector Jeffrey sat. He was a large, very traditional policeman with a solid build and square, uncompromising face. He was bald except for thick tufts of white hair that sprouted over his ears and equally white bushy eyebrows. A thick white moustache, neatly clipped would have completed the picture, but the police force disapproved of moustaches. It would have been such an obvious complement to the hair and eyebrows that his upper lip looked positively naked without it. He looked up as the WRC entered.

"Yes, constable Pratt?" It was fortunate Eileen wasn't there to hear the name. She may have been unable to resist making a comment.

"There's a young lady to see you, sir. She has an appointment for eleven o'clock."

Jeffrey looked at his watch and frowned. "She's early."

"Yes sir, so she said."

The inspector checked with a desk diary. "I see. Miss Chambers, is it?" Pratt shook his head vigorously and held up a warning hand, palm outward. Then he held up one forefinger and used it to draw three imaginary 'V' signs on his arm. Jeffrey stared at him blankly for a moment then laughed. "Ah yes, I understand. A valid distinction, though I don't think you need to be so careful. I'm sure she wouldn't be able to hear you from here. Very well, show Sergeant Chambers in, will you."

Eileen entered a few moments later, and Pratt closed the door behind her leaving the two of them alone. Jeffrey rose politely as she came into the room and indicated a chair on the other side of his desk. "Welcome to Canterbury, Sergeant Chambers - or I gather I should say 'welcome back'. Take a seat. I'd like to ask you to make yourself comfortable but that's impossible on chairs like these." When they were both seated, he went on, "I'm sure you've been given some idea of why we asked you here."

"Not really, I was just given the usual phrase about helping the police with their enquiries. I know my aunt and uncle died in the bombing but I don't understand why any enquiries are necessary. A lot of people must have died that night and I'm sure you're not making enquiries about all of them. We may have been related but we weren't very close, you know."

"I didn't know, as a matter of fact. I know only that you are their closest relative - the next of kin, as it were - and that you lived with them for a short time in Botolph Street before the war."

Eileen shrugged. "That was force of circumstances. My parents died, I hadn't much money and I had to live somewhere. They offered, through a sense of family obligation I suppose, and I accepted. They were the sort of people," she added in a carefully neutral tone, "who took the idea of obligation extremely seriously. In fact, they took just about everything very seriously. They were serious people."

"I see. A case of chalk and cheese, was it?"

"Something like that, yes. But you still haven't explained why I was ordered here."

"Not ordered, sergeant," he protested. "You mustn't call it an order. It was an invitation, that's all."

Eileen smiled. "It may have been an invitation when it originally came from you, inspector, but by the time my officer passed it on to me it had become an order."

"The military mind at work, eh? Let me satisfy your curiosity, if I can. The point is that number thirteen Botolph Street suffered a direct hit. It was an explosive bomb, not an incendiary, and the place was pretty well flattened. The rescue squad found Mr and Mrs Berwick, both dead I'm afraid, but they also found - or rather one of my constables found afterwards - another body in the house."

"That would be very unusual. My aunt and uncle rarely had visitors, only a handful during the time I was there. Also..." She frowned. "Wasn't the raid at night? I read that it started about midnight. They certainly wouldn't have had anyone there at that time of night. It wouldn't have been respectable. Auntie would have been horrified at the thought."

"But this wasn't a visitor. This body had been there for a long time, so long it had become almost a skeleton. When it was found, it was in the cellar."

"I'm getting more and more confused. There wasn't a

13

cellar. I'm sure I would have remembered a cellar door and there wasn't one."

"There was," Jeffrey contradicted her. "The houses in Botolph Street are all of the same design and they all have cellars. If you don't remember one it may be because someone had bricked up the entrance, or perhaps blocked it with some large piece of furniture so it couldn't be seen."

"But why would my uncle do that?"

Jeffrey smiled faintly. "Possibly because there was a body in it, don't you think?"

They sat in silence for a moment, then Eileen said, "This is something of a shock. Do you mind if I smoke?"

"Not at all." He flipped open the lid of a wooden box on his desk and pushed it towards her. "Have one of these."

Eileen thanked him and took a cigarette which the inspector lit for her with a large and expensive looking table lighter. "It was a retirement present, that lighter. I'd retired before the war started. Now here I am, back behind the same old desk. Never mind, other people have to put up with far worse. Now, about this cellar..."

"Yes, I was thinking about that. Do you know where the cellar door would have been?"

"Yes. In those houses the steps down to the cellar lead off the entrance hall. Was there anything in the hall, any wall fittings, coat stand, tall cupboard, anything like that?"

Eileen shook her head. "No, I'm certain there wasn't. It was a very small hallway, there wouldn't have been room for anything of that size." She was quite firm about it. "The door must have been bricked up. Come to think of it, this body must have been down there for a long time before I arrived because the hall hadn't been decorated for quite a few years. Dowdy it was, and quite grubby as I remember."

"Yes, it had been there a very long time. We know that not just because of the state of the remains, but also because the man had been wearing a uniform, an army uniform. There's not much of it left now, of course, but it's still just about recognisable. It wasn't a modern uniform, more the sort of thing we wore in the first war. The buttons and cap badge had lasted better, being brass. They were of the East Kent Regiment - the Buffs, as they're called."

Eileen tapped the ash from her cigarette into the metal ash tray on the desk. She was thinking. Jeffrey, an observant man because of his profession, had already noticed that when she was thinking her eyes narrowed and there was a small frown that puckered her forehead, as if thinking was a very intense activity for her. "But if there was a uniform, wouldn't there also be identity tags? I mean, they were compulsory then as now as far as I know."

He nodded. "Yes. Well spotted. Indeed there were tags." He opened the drawer to the right of his desk and drew out something that he placed on the desktop between them. "Take a look at them, sergeant."

Eileen stubbed out the remnants of her cigarette and picked up the two little tags on their cord. She studied them. They were of the standard pressed fibre type. One was green, the other red. The red one hung on a shorter cord threaded through a hole in the green one. The red tag could be cut off to prove a body had been found, leaving the green one with the body for any future burial party, which was why the religion was always indicated on it. She laid the green tag on the palm of her hand and ran her finger over it. The small thoughtful frown had reappeared. The tags were old, that was obvious. The fibre material lasted quite well, but it would decay eventually. They were, however, still legible with a little effort. She could read the name 'Berwick, D', the service number and CE for Church of England. She looked up.

"They had a son, David. My aunt and uncle, I mean. They hardly ever talked about him but they kept a photograph on the sideboard in the living room. David Berwick. I understood he'd died in the last war and they didn't like the subject to be raised, so I tended to avoid it. So that's who the body was?"

"Possibly."

"Only possibly? Isn't it conclusive? I mean, that's what tags are for, isn't it? To identify bodies."

Jeffrey reached into the still open drawer and picked out something else that he dropped onto the desk as he had the tags. "This was also on the body." Eileen picked it up as she was clearly expected to. It was a chain bracelet with an engraved metal disc hanging from it. As she had done with the fibre tags, Eileen rested it on her palm and read the engraving on the disc: Chase, P followed by the service number and CE. "Soldiers often wore something like that," Jeffrey observed. "They didn't entirely trust the official fibre ones, you see; thought they might rot in the mud. Metal always seems a lot more permanent, doesn't it? So you can see what I mean by 'possibly'. We have two identification tags, but they're for different people. Something of a puzzle."

"Yes." She handed both back to him. He dropped them in the drawer and closed it. "I can see your problem. But I'm afraid I can't be of any help. The other name means nothing to me."

"No. Nor to anyone else, so far. Nobody's heard of Mr Chase, P." He sighed. "Oh well, it was worth asking. We've started enquiries with the War Office and with the regiment but up to now we've had no response."

"I imagine they're rather busy at the moment," Eileen

observed mildly.

"Yes, I've no doubt we'll be a long way down their list of priorities. Quite rightly, of course. Still, we also have our work to do. I'm afraid there ought to be an inquest."

"An inquest? That seems more than a little absurd under the circumstances."

"It does, I agree. However, the law is the law, in peace or in war. In the case of an unexplained death an inquest should be held. The other deaths we're dealing with are far from unexplained, but this one definitely is. I shouldn't think you'll be required for the inquest though, can't see any reason why you should be. The purpose of an inquest is to determine the identity of the deceased and the cause of death, and after having spoken with you I can't see how you could help with either."

"I'm sorry to have disappointed you."

He smiled. "Not at all. I'm the one who should be sorry, to have brought you all this way for nothing. However, we may want to speak to you again before you leave so if you'd be so good as to leave the name of your hotel at the desk..."

"I won't be here long, you know. I only have forty eight hours leave."

"Nevertheless..."

"And I don't have a hotel. I tried to book a room by phone but I haven't found one yet. Not one in a hotel that's still standing, anyway."

"No. Quite. That is a problem at the moment. Never mind, just let us know when you have. If you can't think of anywhere, I'm sure WRC Pratt will be able to recommend somewhere suitable. He's a local lad, knows all the places."

"Thank you." Eileen rose from her chair. "Is that all? If so, I should be going. As I said, only forty eight hours..."

"Yes, that's all for now. I'm grateful for your assistance."

"Such as it was, you're welcome to it." Eileen started for the door but paused and turned with her hand on the doorknob. "Is his name really Pratt?" The corners of her mouth were twitching upwards.

"It is," replied Inspector Jeffrey gravely, with a perfectly straight face.

"Poor boy."

Chapter III

Eileen Chambers was twenty four years old. She had been born in 1918, when the first war had still been a present reality. Her father had fought in it and it had left an indelible mark on him; nothing physical, no bodily wound or scar - he had been lucky in that respect. But there was a mark on his mind, on his emotions. It was there until he died, many years afterwards.

Eileen had never been a particularly pretty child. It wasn't that she was positively ugly or anything like that. She wasn't. She had a firm, well defined face with strong features; the jaw and cheekbones were clear and hard, the lips reasonably full, the skin clear and smooth. There was nothing wrong with her face except that it wasn't exactly... pretty. She became aware of that when she was still quite young. It was obvious from the way some adults fawned over other, prettier and more delicate little girls but didn't treat her in the same way. Then, as she grew older and her body filled out, she didn't become the conventional buxom english rose. Instead she became sturdy, solid... muscular even, more like an athlete rather than anyone's glamourous sweetheart. At that age she had resented the fact, but later she came to accept it. The good part about it was that when she enlisted, the uniform suited her perfectly. She looked naturally at home in it, unlike some of the girls who would have looked more comfortable in frills and lace. Eileen could have been born to wear the severe blue serge tunic and skirt, the wide belt and brass buttons. That was even more true when the training, drill and exercise had firmed her up, trimmed off any excess fat. By then, she was completely in her element. One peculiar aspect of her transformation was that before it she had never particularly attracted male attention, whereas in her uniform, after training, men could sometimes become quite a nuisance - like the merchant seamen in the train that day. It was often said that women were attracted to men in uniform, providing they looked the part. Perhaps the same was true the other way round, just not talked about as much.

The only thing she occasionally regretted was her hair, It had always been the only aspect of her appearance she had ever genuinely been pleased with. It was thick and straw coloured with a natural curl. She was always annoyed when people referred to it - or to her - as blonde. It wasn't blonde at all, or not what most people meant by blonde; blonde conveyed something pale, bland, all too often synthetic. Her hair was more unusual than that, better than that. But now it was wasted, pinned up and tucked underneath the cap according to regulations, almost invisible. Still, she consoled herself, that was a small price to pay.

She had followed the advice of WRC Pratt - a ridiculously apposite name - who had recommended a small hotel on the east side of the city. Quite reasonably priced, he had promised her, and quite clean. He had been right on both counts, somewhat to her surprise. She hadn't bothered to unpack. All she had was her kit bag and taking everything out of it to transfer to drawers seemed completely pointless for the sake of less than forty eight hours. It was all right where it was. She'd just take out the few things she needed when she needed them. In the meantime, she decided to look around the city. She'd known it well once, for a short time, and she wanted to know first hand what had survived the bombing and what had been lost. Also, she thought she'd take a look at

Botolph Street. It had been her home for a while and even though she'd hated it, she felt an impulse to see what was left. She left a message at the hotel desk in case Inspector Jeffrey tried to contact her and stepped out into the June sunshine.

She made for the centre with that confident stride which was more a matter of training than personality. Around her she saw much that was familiar but also much that came as a shock. Many of the old buildings were gone, or if not gone, damaged beyond repair. Sometimes bare, skeletal timbers remained, the wattle and daub filler burnt away by incendiaries but the old hardened oak having resisted the flames. In other cases nothing was left at all, just rubble. The streets were by now largely cleared of debris but there were still people busy amongst the ruins, their activity kicking up clouds of dust that caught in the throat. What would it all look like, she couldn't help wondering, when the dust finally settled? Her walk finally led her, as almost all walks through Canterbury eventually do, along Mercery Lane to Christchurch Gate and the entrance to the cathedral precincts. The lane itself and, mercifully, the gate itself, seemed to have escaped the bombs virtually unscathed. She crossed the little square and passed under the arch of the gate, the cathedral towers looming up as they always had, seemingly unchanged. There was something enormously solid and reassuring about them at a time like this, a time of uncertainty and peril. When she reached the western entrance, however, she received something of a shock. She had intended to go in, to take the opportunity to wander around and relax for a while in the peace and tranquility of the old building - but she couldn't. It would have been impossible.

The floor of the nave was piled high with earth, an uneven heap up to six foot high in places. There were men with shovels, distributing the soil around.

"What the hell," she said out loud, "is going on?"

"Not the most appropriate phrase, under the circumstances." The voice came from behind her. She turned and saw a man in the blue overalls and tin helmet of the ARP. He was grinning, laughing at her. "I reckon 'what in heaven's name' would be better. Holier, like. More in keeping, don't you think?"

"Probably. I wasn't thinking at all, to be honest. It came as a bit of a shock."

"Yes, I imagine it would if you weren't expecting it. Been here before, have you?"

"Yes. A few years ago. I used to live in the city for a short time."

"Where was that, then?" he asked, with the easy confidence of a local who would be able to place any address.

"Botolph Street."

"Ah... There's a coincidence for you. I was there not long ago, on the morning after the raid. You weren't at number thirteen by any chance, were you?"

"I was."

"Oh. Sorry, I didn't know. Bad luck, that. It was the only one to be hit in that street. My name's Alfie, by the way."

Eileen nodded. "Pleased to meet you." But she didn't offer her own name. For some reason, she didn't want to. Instead she reverted to the original subject. "What's this lot all about? Are they trying to bury the place?"

Alfie laughed. "You'd think so, wouldn't you? But no. They're using the crypt as an air raid shelter, you see. It's deep and stone built, so it's a pretty good one. As solid as you can get. But..." he pointed up at the vast, distant vaulted roof over their heads. "If that lot came down on top of it you couldn't guarantee anything. The earth's extra protection, see? A bit of a cushion, you could say, just in case. A pretty big cushion," he added, looking at the clogged nave, "but even so..."

"Yes, I see what you mean. Well, if I can't wander round inside I might as well be going."

"Going to Botolph Street, are you?"

Eileen hadn't actually thought of doing any such thing, but when it was suggested found herself saying, "I may do that, yes."

Alfie nodded sympathetically. "Pay your respects, as it were."

"As it were." She walked off, leaving Alfie standing in the doorway watching her go.

Everything was different, she thought. The whole city was different. Even the apparently eternal and immutable cathedral was different. It was unsettling. It felt as if there was nothing you could rely on, nothing that wouldn't change as soon as you turned your back on it. It was the war, of course. War changed everything.

The walk from the cathedral to Botolph Street should have been familiar; indeed, much of it was. She had followed the same route every weekday for nearly two tedious years. Two years were a long time when you were that age. After moving in with her aunt and uncle, she had found a job at a surveyor's office in the city and the short journey from home to office and back had become a habit, something she hadn't needed to think about but had followed as a matter of course. Now, though, the old familiarity was constantly jolted by some missing building or some charred ruin where there used to be a house or a shop; the gaps were like gaps not in rows of buildings but in her memory, as if she had somehow got things wrong, had misremembered.

The job had been boring but necessary. Mainly it was because she had needed the money, but in addition to that it had provided an excuse to get out of the tightly regulated prison of thirteen Botolph Street. A surveyor's office, however monotonous and uninteresting it may have been, had been infinitely preferable to the claustrophobic respectability of her aunt and uncle's house. She'd hoped at first the money may enable her to escape, to rent a place of her own, but it had never been enough. That was in part because the Berwicks' sense of family obligation had never stretched so far as to allow her to live rent free; she had always had to contribute to her upkeep, as her aunt delicately put it. After what she gave to them, there was never enough left from her wages to finance an independent existence.

Water under the bridge, she thought firmly as she strode along the streets. It was all behind her now. When the war came and the armed forces started recruiting women, she hadn't hesitated. It had been a godsend. She'd gone to the recruiting office, taken an immediate dislike to the ATS uniform, decided the WRNS was no good on the irrational grounds that she couldn't swim, and so signed her name for the WAAF. It had been that absurdly simple. There had been no dithering, no weighing of consequences, no doubts; she'd just gone ahead and done it. And she'd never regretted it.

Well... perhaps not quite true. There had been moments in the early days, crammed into a hut with too many other girls most of whom were younger than her, with the uncomfortable 'biscuit' mattresses and the concrete troughs with enamel bowls for washing - cold water only, of course - yes, there had been moments when she'd wondered whether she'd done the right thing. Especially when she first saw the underwear they were issued to wear beneath the smart uniform. That had been a source of incredulous amusement for all of them. But the doubts hadn't lasted long. She'd settled in, become accustomed to being shouted at by NCOs, adapted to the

24

monotony of drill and parades, made friends amongst the other girls and decided that really, despite everything, the life quite suited her. She'd done the right thing. And perhaps more than anything else, she'd succeeded by her own efforts in escaping from Botolph Street.

And it hadn't changed. When she turned into the street, everything was exactly the same, as featureless and blandly respectable as she remembered it. Except that... Except that, of course, number thirteen wasn't there any more. She stood facing the wreckage, oddly feeling nothing, just wondering what she *should* feel, what would be appropriate. There should be something, surely. Not regret, not sorrow, but *something*, even if it were just a reprehensible pleasure or satisfaction. But no. Nothing.

Just as she remembered, the street was almost deserted. It always had been. The people there weren't sociable, they stayed in their houses or they were out at work. They didn't chat over the neat hedges or pop in to see one another, stop off for a neighbourly cup of tea or an exchange of gossip. And it wasn't on the way from anywhere to anywhere else, so people who didn't live there rarely passed through. Now, she could see an elderly man further down the street tending a tiny, fussy little front garden and studiously ignoring her, and there was a woman carrying a shopping bag walking slowly up the street towards her. Those were the only signs of human activity. It was dead. That had been her overwhelming impression at the time and she thought the same now.

The only other sign of life wasn't human, it was canine; there was a dog sitting on the rubble, looking down at her, its head tilted to one side. She stared back at it, wondering who it belonged to. There hadn't been any dogs on Botolph Street when she had been there. Probably none of the residents would have wanted anything so untidy as a dog - and if they had, it would have been some sort of small clean and presentable pedigree animal, which this one definitely wasn't.

"Funny, isn't it?" The woman with the shopping bag had stopped next to her. "That dog's been turning up every now and then ever since the raid. I'd never seen it before that, I swear I hadn't. I'd remember. Don't know where it comes from."

She was a middle aged woman, perhaps in her forties, pink and plump and fleshy with curly hair that was just beginning to show traces of grey. She wore a summer dress with a bold floral print, appropriate for the weather but far too brash for the shape of her body and somehow at odds with all of the destruction Eileen had seen recently. It was just too cheerful, too normal.

"Sorry, you don't know me. I haven't introduced myself. My name's Charlotte Baines, spinster of this parish." She giggled like a schoolgirl. "I always say that. Silly, isn't it? Anyway, everybody always calls me Lottie."

"Yes, I know. You live just around the corner, don't you? I remember you."

"Do you? How flattering. But I'm afraid I don't remember you." She was a short woman, and looked up at Eileen inquisitively. "Have you been here before?"

"Yes. I lived here for a short time. Before the war."

"What... you mean *here*? Right here? At number thirteen?"

"That's right."

Lottie stared at her, then suddenly recognition dawned. "Oh yes! You were the Berwicks' niece, weren't you? My, how you've changed! I wouldn't have known you." She looked Eileen up and down with frank admiration. "You're like a different person. So confident now, so smart."

Eileen couldn't help but smile at the innocent compliment. "Thank you."

26

"Not at all. Lottie speaks as she finds, everybody knows that. They may not all like it, but they know it. You were a grumpy young thing in those days, always miserable and bad tempered. Not surprising I suppose, considering the company you had to keep."

Eileen laughed. "You weren't keen on my aunt and uncle, then?"

"That's putting it mildly. They didn't like Lottie and Lottie didn't like them. Stuck up, they were, self-righteous if you don't mind me saying so."

"I don't mind at all. I thought the same."

"I don't want to speak ill of the dead, but... Well, perhaps I'd best say nothing at all. If you can't think of anything good to say, don't say anything." She giggled again. "My old mother used to say that. She used to say a lot of things, most of them were rubbish but some were sensible. She's gone now, of course. Died years ago. Still, never mind. Everybody dies, don't they?"

"Yes, they do."

"Talking of dying," Lottie was in full flow now, "I'm told they found another body when they tried to rescue your aunt and uncle."

"Who told you that?"

"The police. They came round asking questions, but I didn't tell them anything. That's another thing my old mother used to say - don't tell the police any more than you have to, it only makes trouble."

Eileen was intrigued. "Could you have told them anything? If you'd wanted to, I mean."

"Perhaps I could and perhaps I couldn't. Who knows? They certainly don't." Another giggle. "Anyway, I must be going now. But while you're here, drop round some time for a cup of tea. I don't get many visitors these days. Lottie's not very popular, not like she used to be when she was younger."

"I will," Eileen lied, in order to please.

Lottie started to walk away, then impulsively turned back. "If you do," she said, "I might tell you what I didn't tell the police. There's an incentive for you."

Eileen watched her walk away then turned to look at the ruin again. It was exactly the same except that the dog had vanished.

Chapter IV

When she got back to her hotel, Eileen was tired. Why was it, she wondered, that walking around towns tired you more than walking anywhere else? It wasn't the distance, which was nothing really. She couldn't be bothered to work it out, so went straight to the reception desk to pick up her room key. The desk wasn't actually a physical desk but was a small enclosed area with its own door, a cubicle with a glass front. Inside it, a lugubrious old man with a walrus moustache sat behind the counter with a bored but patient expression. He must, she thought, have very little to do all day.

"Are there any messages for me?" She ought to ask, in case the police had been trying to contact her. "Chambers, Sergeant Chambers."

He looked her up and down, taking in the uniform with its stripes on the sleeve. "I'd have guessed that without you telling me. No, no messages."

"Thank you." Eileen turned to leave.

"However..." She sighed and turned back. The old man sat there, expressionless, looking at her.

"Yes?" He seemed to need prompting.

"However, there is somebody waiting to see you."

"Who?"

"I don't know. A man. He didn't give a name. He's been here about half an hour, sitting in the residents' lounge. I thought that was acceptable because although he's not a resident, you are. That makes him a sort of resident by proxy, if you see what I mean. No harm in it anyway, I thought."

"No harm at all, I'm sure." Jobsworth, she thought.

"Besides, there's nowhere else for him to wait."

"No."

What was rather grandly known as the residents' lounge was a small room off the entrance hall, almost directly opposite the desk. It was furnished like the parlour of a domestic house, with armchairs, sofas and low tables. The intention must have been to make it appear comfortable and cosy. In fact, there was too much furniture for the size of the room which just made it cramped and cluttered. You had to imitate a slalom event just to make your way round the obstacles. A selection of very proper and respectable newspapers and magazines were spread over the tables for the edification of any residents bored enough to resort to reading them. The sole occupant of the room was ensconced in a large padded armchair with a straight pipe in his mouth though it appeared not to be alight and was, whether through sheer boredom or for some other reason, perusing one of the magazines. It was an old edition of *The Field*, Eileen noticed. He was a very ordinary looking man, small and plain; if asked, she would have had trouble describing him simply because there were no remarkable or outstanding features. He had a round, rather bland face, shiny and clean shaven; slightly thinning, wispy hair; and he wore a nondescript creased grey suit that looked as if he'd had it since before the war. She carefully threaded her way through the furnishings until she stood next to him. He lifted his head and smiled at her. A friendly smile, amiable and natural, that rounded his cheeks and made crinkles around the corners of his eyes.

"You're waiting to see me, I gather."

"Sergeant Chambers, I assume. Yes I am. Just passing the time by learning how the other half live." He dropped the magazine back on the table in front of him.

"Remarkable, isn't it? Reading this, you'd think nothing had changed. Mind you, I haven't looked at the date. It could be pre-war."

"It wouldn't surprise me." Eileen sat down opposite him. The seat of the armchair sagged beneath her leaving her lower than she had expected. "Are you from the police?"

He laughed. "Good heavens, no! Do I look like a policeman?" He sounded quite anxious at the thought.

"Not much. Does that mean you weren't sent by Inspector Jeffrey?"

"Sent? Yes I was, in a way. He certainly knows I'm here. He told me where to find you. A nice man, don't you think? Missing his retirement, it seems to me."

"Yes. So you're not a policeman, but the police know you're here. You're being a little mysterious, aren't you?"

"Me?" He looked surprised at the suggestion. "No, no, no, not mysterious at all. Perhaps just a little vague. I can be vague sometimes, or so I'm told. My name's Ragley, by the way. I already know yours and I wouldn't want you to be at a disadvantage."

"So who exactly are you, Mr Ragley?"

"Ah well..." He looked down at the bowl of his pipe, frowned, took out a box of matches and proceeded to relight it, and exercise that took several seconds and enveloped him in a temporary cloud of smoke. "Well, *exactly*, I work for Military Intelligence. We do work with the police, naturally, but we're not part of them. Entirely different kettle of fish."

"Yes, I know. I've had dealings with Military Intelligence from time to time."

"You would have, of course. Vetting, that sort of thing."

"That's right." Eileen was becoming cautious. Ragley was both ordinary and odd at one and the same time.

"You're quite right to be cautious," he said as if he'd read her mind. "Quite right. You'd like to see some identification, no doubt. Very sensible of you." He fished in an inside pocket and came out with a piece of paper that he flourished with the air of a conjuror producing a rabbit from a hat. "Here you are, all official and above board."

Eileen took it and stared at it for a moment. "I see. They wouldn't be all that difficult to forge, would they?"

Ragley smiled. "No, I'm afraid not. I'm told the Abwehr can come up with a quite reasonable facsimile, though I've never actually seen one."

Eileen was still scanning the little document. "Department Five? What's that, anyway?"

"Oh, you know. It's just a department. All government bodies have departments, don't they? Like commercial companies. It makes them feel important. I can understand you being a little dubious." He took the paper back and abruptly changed the subject. "Tell me, sergeant, where are you stationed at the moment?"

"I can't tell you that. You should know I can't." Eileen was indignant.

"Quite so. Naturally you can't. It's secret information, isn't it? Very sensitive. Nobody must know." He put the identification back in his pocket and puffed ruminatively on his pipe. Eventually he went on. "Currently you're at Rudloe Manor, control centre for number ten fighter group. You work in the filter room there. It must be a great strain, that work," he added sympathetically, "constant concentration, good judgement, quick decisions that may have lives depending on them... Very tiring, I should think. I couldn't do it myself."

Eileen looked around the room desperately. "For heaven's sake..."

Ragley laughed. "Yes, I know. Careless talk costs lives; be like dad, keep mum. Walls have ears and all that sort of thing. Most commendable, but I doubt these particular walls have any ears and there's nobody else about. Your initial training," he continued, unperturbed, "was in Bridgenorth. Then you transferred to Cranwell for technical training in radar... Do you want me to go on?"

"No!" Eileen almost shouted the word. Ragley looked amused.

"It's all right. I have a quiet voice and there's no one listening. It's too easy to get carried away with these things nowadays. One needs to be careful, yes, but also one should be realistic. Keep a sense of proportion. The point is, are you more convinced than you were by my ID papers?"

"Yes. How do you know these things?"

"Oh, I do a little homework, you know." He sounded pleased with himself, but modest. "And I have access to some documents that most people don't, which is rather an unfair advantage."

"But what I don't understand is why you or your people should be interested in David Berwick. That was his name, wasn't it? David? He was just another casualty of the last war, wasn't he? One of thousands."

"Yes that was his name. And it was hundreds of thousands, to be pedantic about it. I'm told I can be quite pedantic, I'm afraid. But actually we're not interested in him at all. We're interested in Paul Chase."

It took Eileen a few seconds to place the name. "The identity bracelet. You believe the body was him, then?"

"We don't know. But we would definitely like to know, one way or the other. We have an interest in Mr Chase."

"Why?"

"Ah well..." He smiled, a disarming, harmless smile on the round face. "To borrow your own words, I'm not allowed to tell you that. Frustrating, isn't it?" He took the pipe from his mouth, frowned down at the bowl then knocked it out on the ash tray. "Tobacco doesn't seem to last as long as it used to. Wartime economy, I expect. The thing is, sergeant, I'd like to know about that body, and particularly about its identity. And I rather hope you'll be able to help me."

"That's more or less what Inspector Jeffrey said, but I honestly don't see how I can help anyone. It's as much a mystery to me as to anybody else. I told Jeffrey so."

"Yes, I know. He passed that on to me. The thing is..." It seemed to be a favourite phrase of his. "The thing is, you're local here - or at least you were for a short time. People will remember you. They may talk to you, tell you things they wouldn't tell anyone official. The police have knocked on doors and asked questions, of course, but they got nowhere. I don't suppose I'd get any further, do you? Can you imagine any of the neighbours gossiping to me?"

Eileen recalled Lottie's comment - don't tell the police any more than you have to, it only makes trouble. "No, I can't," she admitted.

"Me, even less than the police. At least they'll be familiar with local constables, they'll have seen them before. And the uniform is quite reassuring, isn't it? But I'd just be some nosey anonymous government busybody. That's how you may be able to help, sergeant - just by talking to people. Would you be willing to do that?"

"Do I have any choice?"

"Of course you do. I'm not your superior officer, I can't order you to do anything even if I wanted to. I'm just asking for your assistance." He waited, expectantly.

"Well..." Eileen felt a strange reluctance. "I'll do anything I can to help, naturally. But really I don't hold out much hope. Besides anything else, there just wouldn't be enough time. I only have forty eight hours leave, you know."

Ragley raised his eyebrows. "Is that all? No, I didn't know. You're right. though, that wouldn't be anywhere near long enough. Oh no, not at all. We'll have to do something about that."

"I'd love to, believe me, but I'm afraid we can't. That's all the leave I've been given."

Ragley took out an oilskin tobacco pouch and began to refill his pipe. He was very slow and methodical about it, seemingly absorbed in what he was doing. "Yes," he said at last, "it is a problem, isn't it. But you would be *willing* to help, if you could?"

"If I could, yes of course. But..."

"I know. Forty eight hours, not enough. How about a week? That would be enough, I should think."

"I told you, I don't have a week."

Ragley lit his pipe, disappearing again in a cloud of smoke. "Don't worry about that, I'll arrange it. We'll say a week then, shall we?"

"You can't really do that, can you?"

"Oh, I think so. I'm pretty certain of it, in fact. Anyway, a week's break from that demanding work will do you good, give you a chance to relax a little. I'm sure you've deserve it. Yes, a week." He took the pipe from his mouth and smiled benignly at her. "The paperwork should be with you by tomorrow morning. If it doesn't arrive for some reason, call your commanding officer. Baker, isn't it? A very capable man, I'm told. He'll confirm it." Eileen stared at him, open mouthed. He stood up, apparently unconscious of her reaction, and picked up his hat which had been lying on the table. "I'll be in touch, sergeant. If you need to contact me, the police station will be able to find me. Otherwise, just see what if anything you can discover for me." He smiled amiably. "And enjoy your leave."

35

Chapter V

Eileen didn't go out that evening, she stayed in her room. It was no fun wandering about a town in the blackout, especially when that town had recently been bombed and still had rubble lying everywhere to twist the ankles of the unwary. The blackout was a gift for people who didn't want to be seen; it was a criminal's paradise. For everybody else it was an annoyance at best and a danger at worst. So Eileen decided to stay in her room and read. She had stowed a novel in her kit bag, a detective story. She levered off her shoes (military shoes weren't the sort that could easily be kicked off), lay on the bed and opened the book but somehow found she couldn't concentrate on it. It just seemed silly and far-fetched, with cardboard cut out characters and a ridiculously implausible plot. Surely no one who wanted to murder somebody would do it like that - there must be simpler ways. Her mind kept straying from the story until eventually she gave it up as a bad job and dropped the book onto the bedside table.

Lying on her back with her ankles crossed and hands behind her head, she thought about what had happened that day. It was all very puzzling. She still wasn't entirely sure why the police had requested her presence or what she could do to help them. That the station had granted her forty eight hours leave at the request of the police was understandable but she couldn't imagine why the police had requested it in the first place. There hadn't been anything that couldn't have been settled by a short telephone call. And then there was Ragley...

The whole thing, she suspected, had been organised by him from the beginning. He wouldn't tell her what military intelligence had to do with it, but then that was perfectly typical of military intelligence. They never told anyone anything if they could possibly avoid it, they were notorious for it. He was, she thought, a very mild inoffensive sort of man - or at least he gave that impression, which may have been deliberate.

What, really, did he want of her? The police request may have been puzzling, but Ragley had been positively baffling. Talk to people, see if anyone tells you anything... That, when you came down to it, was all he had said. It was silly. She wasn't qualified for that sort of thing. He'd made a point of her being local, but she wasn't. She never had been. A brief and resentful residence was all it had been. And if the neighbours wouldn't talk to an official like Ragley, would they be any more likely to talk to a woman in uniform?

But then she remembered Lottie. Lottie had been willing to talk, hadn't she? Perhaps there was something in it after all.

She was tired now, and thinking of Lottie made her think of her time in Botolph Street, setting her mind drifting over old memories. It hadn't been a good time. She had been nineteen when she moved in with her aunt and uncle - nineteen and still smarting from the unexpected death of her parents, still feeling a little lost and bewildered. She'd had a sheltered upbringing in some ways, been spoiled you could say; an only child of doting parents. When they were suddenly taken away, the shock was tremendous. They'd left her virtually no money and nothing valuable. Even the house she'd occupied with them had been rented, and within a very short time she discovered she couldn't afford the rent. She hadn't known what to do or where to go. She'd been pathetically grateful when the Berwicks had offered her a home, but it hadn't been long before she knew she'd made a mistake.

Aunt Edna and uncle George: that was what they'd liked her to call them. Probably they liked it because it reinforced the idea of family obligation that they set such store by. George didn't say much and what he did say was mostly just to agree with Edna. He gave the general impression that he regarded talking to women as a waste of time. Edna, on the other hand, talked a lot.

"I don't know why you're not married." That was almost the first thing she said to Eileen after her arrival. "A girl of your age ought to be married, or at least have somebody in mind. I'd been married for two years when I was your age"

Yes, Eileen thought, married to George. That in itself should have been enough to settle the issue of the desirability of marriage. But all she said was, "I don't really want to get married, aunt Edna. Anyway, I've never met anybody I wanted to marry."

"That's not the point."

"Isn't it?"

"No." No, of course it wasn't. To begin with, Eileen hadn't understood that. The point was respectability, convention, doing what was expected. What you wanted didn't come into it. She had started off trying to argue but that was before she discovered that arguing with Edna was a completely wasted effort. It was like arguing with a brick wall. Edna didn't argue, all she did was repeat the same thing over and over again with slight variations in phrasing, as if the more often you said something, the more true it became. George, of course, simply agreed with her or said nothing. Most often he said nothing.

Edna was her mother's sister, an older sister. They hadn't met often before Eileen moved to Canterbury, so she hadn't much idea of what to expect. Perhaps she had expected someone similar to her mother, some family resemblance, but there was no similarity at all either in appearance or in temperament. It had come as a shock, a shock to be added onto the other shocks Eileen had experienced recently.

When she managed to get a job, she fully believed Aunt Edna would object, but all she said was, "Well at least it's a respectable job, in an office. It's not as if you're going to become a shop girl or a waitress or anything of that kind. Of course, a woman shouldn't have go out to work at all but as you don't have a husband to look after you... It might even be a good thing. You might meet a suitable man, somebody with good prospects. That would be welcome," she appealed to male authority, "wouldn't it, George?"

"Yes dear." That was George's usual contribution to any discussion.

She hadn't met a suitable man, of course; not one *she* considered suitable though her aunt would probably have disagreed. Edna disagreed with almost anything, as a matter of principle. There were a couple of men in the office who tried their luck, as some men always do, but Eileen wasn't interested. Besides, she would have been very surprised if either of them had anything as decorous as marriage in mind.

And so it went on, not getting any better, until the war started and Eileen enlisted. At that point her life, which she'd felt had been more or less on hold since the death of her parents, began again. A new life and as far as she was concerned, a better one. She hadn't heard from the Berwicks since she left their house, and she had made no attempt to contact them. She had been glad to be rid of them and suspected the feeling was mutual. But now, thanks to the violent intervention of the Luftwaffe, here she was again in Canterbury, lying in bed and thinking about them. She sighed and tucked herself up beneath the blankets. Enough dwelling on the past. It was time for sleep.

She was woken up less than two hours later. At first, still drowsy and befuddled, in a strange room in the dark, she couldn't work out what had woken her. Then the obvious noise penetrated the haze of sleep and she recognised the undulating banshee wail of air raid sirens.

Damn!

It was tempting just to turn over, put the pillows over her head and stay where she was. However... No, she couldn't do that. She had a responsibility. A sergeant had to set an example.

Grumbling mentally to herself, she started to pull on her uniform. Uniform buttons could be a bloody nuisance when you were in a hurry.

Ignoring the sirens, she thought, was exactly what her aunt and uncle had done - and look where it had got them. She could almost imagine the conversation they'd had in bed that night.

"Are you awake, dear?"

"Obviously I'm awake. Nobody could sleep through that, could they?"

"Then we should getting to the shelter."

"I'm not going out through the garden to that shelter, not dressed like this. It wouldn't be proper. I'm staying where I am."

"Yes dear."

That would have been aunt Edna. Propriety would take precedence over safety any time. It took precedence over everything.

Fully dressed now, Eileen grabbed her gas mask case and headed for the door. At least the hotel had its own shelter, in the cellars, so she wouldn't have to walk the streets or hide in the cathedral crypt. Perhaps it would turn out to be a false alarm and she'd be back in bed within half an hour, you never knew. Then, just as she reached the door, she heard the distinctive pom-pom thudding of Bofors anti-aircraft guns not very far away. Probably, she thought, they were in the barracks to the east of the city. She paused for a moment to listen, and beneath the sound of the guns she thought she could detect the monotonous throbbing drone of aircraft engines; heavy aircraft. Bombers.

It wasn't a false alarm. High time she was in the cellars.

Chapter VI

The following morning, Eileen stopped off at the desk before going in to breakfast.

"Anything for me?" The old man with the thick moustache was there again. He seemed to be permanently in residence in the little cubicle. He reached back to the wooden pigeon holes on the wall and took out two envelopes, handing them to her wordlessly. "Was there much damage done last night? It didn't seem to last all that long."

"I couldn't say, not first hand. I haven't heard about much, though, not compared to last time."

Eileen took the letters with her to the breakfast room and laid them on the table. She would open them over breakfast.

The first turned out to be from Inspector Jeffrey, a short but polite note informing her that if she cared to drop in to the police station at some time convenient to her, he had some news that may be of interest. Eileen smiled at the courteous but careful wording. The traditional British police, she thought, just as they should be but sometimes weren't. She put the letter away and opened the other one. It contained two pieces of paper, held together by a paper clip.

The top sheet was a leave document, with the station stamp in the top right hand corner and the usual indecipherable scrawl in the space for the signature at the bottom. She looked at the 'to' and 'from' dates. Yes, unbelievably it was seven days. Not only that, but seven days starting from when her current forty eight hours expired, so seven *extra* days. Ragley, she thought, despite his bland undistinguished appearance and unassuming manner, must be able to pull strings in some very high places. She'd been cynical about it, but it turned out she'd been wrong.

She removed the paper clip and looked at the other sheet. It was a scrap of writing paper, pulled from a pad and torn in half so it would fit behind the leave document. On it was written in a round, feminine hand, 'Some people have all the luck! J.'. Eileen laughed out loud, drawing curious looks from the few other people in the room.

'J' would be Jessie. Aircraftswoman Jessie Cumberland dealt with the outgoing post. She was expressly forbidden from interfering with the post in any way on pain of disciplinary procedures, but Jessie was a determinedly cheerful product of Roedean and some Swiss finishing school who had a notoriously casual attitude towards discipline and rank. Women like her could be a pain in the neck, but they could also sometimes bring a welcome touch of levity to what was otherwise a hard and exhausting job. That little note would have to be disposed off without anyone else seeing it.

After breakfast Eileen would have to visit the police station and also see what she could do - if anything - for Ragley. She decided Ragley would come first. She owed him that for misjudging him and above all for the extra week's leave.

So she found herself once again in Botolph Street. As she passed the ruins of number thirteen automatically looked out for the scruffy dog, but it was nowhere to be seen. She couldn't remember exactly where Lottie lived. She knew it was in a side street that went off to the left, but she couldn't recall the number. She turned into the street and started off along it. The houses were different here; there were none of the neat little gardens of Botolph

Street. The houses were terraced and the front doors opened directly onto the street. As she walked, a memory came back to her.

Aunt Edna had never had any time for Lottie. Lottie just wasn't respectable enough. "That woman," she'd said, "is half witted. And when she was young her morals were disgusting. Her mother was no better, god rest her soul. It's a bad family. You should stay away from her, Eileen. Don't have anything to do with her." And then the relevant part. "You can't mistake her house. It's the dirtiest one in the street. Heaven knows when she last washed her curtains or cleaned her windows, let alone scrubbed her doorstep. It's a disgrace, that's what it is."

So: look for the dirtiest house in the street, if Edna was right. And in matters like that, matters that involved the proprieties, she usually was. Eileen walked down the street. There was indeed a house whose frontage was noticeably scruffier than most. It wasn't anywhere near as extreme as aunt Edna had made out, but that was only to be expected. Nevertheless, it had a down at heel look, an overall air of neglect. The windows were grubby, the paintwork faded and in places peeling. The brickwork was in dire need of pointing and there were a couple of tiles missing from the roof. The guttering sagged and quite probably leaked in wet weather.

That must be the one.

Eileen knocked on the door and waited. Lottie may be out, of course, shopping or whatever else she did. However, she wasn't out; after a few moments the door opened and the plump round face peered out at her. Lottie was wearing a floral apron bearing old, indelible stains. Its strings were wrapped twice around her ample waist imparting something of the look of an untidily bundled parcel.

"Oh, it's you. I wondered if I'd see you, hoped I

44

would. Come in, come in."

Eileen stepped inside. The front door opened directly into a living room, with no hallway in between. The room was crowded with furniture. There was a three piece suite that took up most of the available space, and somehow an old sideboard had also been fitted in. Two pot plants, both of them looking irretrievably dead, stood on the sideboard. Another in a similar state occupied the window ledge though it hadn't been visible from the outside because of the grime on the window panes. The mantlepiece was overburdened with painted pottery ornaments, all very old souvenirs from some holiday resort or other.

"Sit yourself down and make yourself comfortable. You may have to move something from the chairs, but just throw it on the floor. Lottie's not very tidy, I'm afraid, never has been. I'll go and make a pot of tea. I'm sure you'd like a cup, wouldn't you?"

"Thank you, yes I would." Eileen picked up some tangled knitting and a half unravelled ball of wool from one of the armchairs, dropped it on the floor as instructed and sat down. The seat subsided beneath her alarmingly as if it were on the verge of collapse. Lottie disappeared through a door on the opposite side of the room, presumably to the kitchen. There was the sound of a tap running and the metallic clatter of kettle and teapot.

"I know why you've come." The voice floated out from the kitchen. "It wasn't because you wanted to see Lottie, was it? It was because you wanted to hear my old gossip. Gossip from years ago, not new gossip. That's right, isn't it?"

"Well..."

"Of course it is. Lottie knows. There's no need to feel embarrassed about it. Everybody likes a bit of gossip and when you're my age, old gossip is always more interesting than new gossip."

After a few minutes, she reappeared carrying a tray with teapot, milk jug, and cups and saucers. She stood in the middle of the room, looking round, but there was no surface on which she could put the tray.

"Oh dear. Well, it doesn't matter, does it?" She put the tray down on the floor then cleared another chair and sat down. "The milk's out of a tin, I'm afraid. It always is these days. Now, do you want to be mother or shall I?" Suddenly she giggled. "That's a silly thing to say. Neither of us is a mother, are we? Both of us are spinsters and Lottie's an old maid into the bargain. Never mind, I'll pour." She did, awkwardly because of the position of the tray on the floor, and handed Eileen the cup and saucer. Eileen sipped. The tea was awful, strong and bitter, not helped by the viscous and sickly sweet condensed milk.

"Thank you. That's very welcome," she lied politely. "Now, you were talking about old gossip..."

"That's right, I was. David Berwick. You'd be too young to remember him, of course. And even if you weren't, he'd been long gone by the time you came here. But I knew him. He was about the same age as me, give or take a couple of years. The police came round asking about him. They wouldn't say, naturally, but I guessed they thought the body they found at number thirteen might have been his. They never tell you things like that, but you can guess easily enough, can't you? Why else would they be asking about him after all these years?

"He was a nice young man, was David. Handsome, too. I liked him, and he liked me. I know he did, because he told me so more than once. His parents didn't approve, of course. The Berwicks never had any time for Lottie. I wasn't good enough. Too common for them, Lottie was. David wasn't like his parents, though. He had a mind of his own. It led to a few arguments in the family, that did, but he didn't let that stop him. Looking back, I suppose the one thing he had in common with his mum and dad was that he tended to take everything quite seriously, didn't laugh enough. Even so, he liked Lottie and he wasn't going to let them change his mind. Quite taken with me, he was, though I shouldn't be the one to say it. At the time I thought... well, if there hadn't been the war we might have... Wishful thinking, I expect. Anyway, there *was* the war, and there it is. Mustn't grumble over spilt milk, must we? Talking of milk, would you like some more tea?"

Eileen refused politely but firmly. She couldn't face any more of that coagulated liquid.

"Anyway, David came home on leave in 1916. I knew he was coming because he'd written to tell me. I don't suppose he ever told his parents he wrote to Lottie, but he did just the same. Silly little letters they were, not saying much, but I shouldn't think he had any choice about that. He probably wanted to say more but the letters were all censored, just like they are now, so you couldn't say much. But I'm rambling again. The point is, I knew he was coming even though I didn't know exactly when, so I took to waiting outside the station. Canterbury East, it was. I guessed it would be that one because he'd be coming from one of the channel ports and all those lines go to Canterbury East. I spent a lot of time waiting and very boring it was too, but in the end it turned out be worth it because I was there when he arrived. I had a surprise though, because he had a friend with him. That was Paul Chase.

"They were in the same regiment and it turned out they both had leave at the same time. Great chums, they were. They looked a bit alike as well, both of them tall and dark haired, the same sort of build. They could almost have been brothers when you first saw them. Not when you got to know them, of course, but that was different. Looking alike doesn't mean behaving alike, does it? They couldn't have been more different in that way. David was always polite, always a bit of a gentleman if you see what I mean; Paul was... well, he was a bit of a lad. A bit cheeky." She giggled again. "Very cheeky, sometimes. You may not believe it, but Lottie was quite a looker in those days. Oh yes, she attracted the boys, did Lottie, did it without even trying. Paul was attracted, and David didn't like it. You could tell."

"But none of that matters, does it? Not now. The thing is, they were both here in 1916. Paul was always talking about his family, his home, his dogs. It was all he talked about, really, but for some reason he couldn't go back there. There'd been some family trouble, I think, though I didn't like to ask. Anyway, David had said to him: come and stay with me during our leave, then. What his parents thought about it when they found out, I can't imagine. It's not something they'd have wanted. On the other hand, in those days you couldn't refuse shelter to a soldier. It would have been unpatriotic, that would. So I suppose they just had to put up with it, for the sake of appearances if nothing else. That was them, wasn't it? Anything for the sake of appearances.

"So they were both there, David Berwick and Paul Chase, both there at the same time. Then one day, when their leave was over, they both disappeared. I didn't see them go, even though I knew their leave was up and I waited at the station to say goodbye. No, they just both disappeared." Lottie looked up slyly. "Or perhaps only one of them did. That's what it looks like now, isn't it?"

"Yes," Eileen agreed slowly. "Yes, that's what it looks like. I wonder which one it was. Who stayed and who went away?"

Chapter VII

"You won't tell the police, will you? I don't want the police round here again."

That had been the last thing Lottie had said before Eileen left. Eileen had done her best to be reassuring but evasive. She was due to see Inspector Jeffrey later, so she would have to make up her mind one way or the other. It was surprisingly difficult, much more difficult than it should have been. Naturally she should tell the police, it was her duty. On the other hand... Lottie had confided in her precisely because she *wasn't* the police, or any sort of legal authority. Despite her uniform, to Lottie she was just the woman who had lived round the corner in Botolph Street. She didn't want to get Lottie into any kind of trouble.

Also, Ragley complicated everything.

She had to tell him, of course. There could be no doubt about that. It was because of him she had been there in the first place, carrying out his instructions to ask around, find out what she could. If she didn't tell him, there would have been no point in finding out anything. Besides, she owed him for an extra week's leave. And there was something about quiet, unassuming Ragley that made one inclined to trust him. He would never be heavy handed about anything, never oppressively official or bullying. He just wasn't the type. Or perhaps it was just that he was clever enough to give that impression, and she was being taken for a fool. She didn't know, could only trust her instincts.

One thing was certain, though; if she told Military

Intelligence (in the unlikely guise of Mr Ragley) there was surely no need to tell the civilian police as well. She would have done her duty and reported the matter. If the two authorities didn't talk to one another, that was no business of hers. She herself was military not civilian, so that was the route she would take. There would be no need to lie to the police, which would have been an entirely different matter. She would simply say nothing at all.

It was only gossip after all, wasn't it?

As things turned out, Inspector Jeffrey didn't ask. He wanted to see her only to keep her informed.

"There's been a post mortem examination. It's a bit late, but the police surgeons have been too busy with the living lately to spare much time for the dead. However, someone has finally got round to it and I thought you may like to hear his conclusions. They do concern you, in a way, as someone who used to know the Berwicks." He picked up a little sheaf of papers that had been lying on his desk, held together at the corner by a treasury tag. He scanned each sheet in turn until he came to the last one. "This is really the only significant part. The body had suffered from a severe depressed fracture of the parietal bone. In the absence of soft tissue It's impossible to say with certainty that this was the cause of death, but if he wasn't dead already it would definitely have been sufficient to kill him." He looked up at Eileen. "These people have a language of their own. Would you like me to translate?"

"No, I don't think so. Someone had bashed him over the head very hard. That's what it means, isn't it?"

Jeffrey smiled. "Very succinctly put. Yes, that's about the size of it. Unfortunately that means there will have to be an inquest. There's no getting away from it. It's a nuisance for me but the good news as far as you're concerned is that I can't see any reason why your presence would be required. You can return to your duties once your forty eight hours is up, and you should never hear from me again."

"As a matter of fact..." Eileen hesitated, unsure how much to say. "My leave has been extended."

Jeffrey raised his thick bushy eyebrows, with an effect that was almost comical. "Has it, indeed? That's very fortunate for you. I congratulate you. I wonder why it happened. May I ask, did our Mr Ragley have anything to do with it, do you think?"

"Yes, he did."

Jeffrey nodded and sat back in his chair, clasping his hands over his stomach. It was a contemplative sort of pose. "An odd cove isn't he, our Mr Ragley? Decidedly odd. An ordinary looking chap, on the surface. Nobody would tell me much about him, but I suspect he's more important than you'd imagine."

"I'm sure he is. Getting someone's leave extended at short notice isn't something just anybody could do."

"No. Quite."

"And there's another odd thing." Eileen had only just thought of the idea, and came out with it impulsively. "You call him *Mr* Ragley, and I think of him like that as well. But he's Military Intelligence, isn't he? He must have a rank, surely. I wonder what it is?"

"I don't know, he never uses it."

"A lot higher than mine, anyway," Eileen admitted ruefully. "Never mind. Actually, I need to contact him and he said that you..."

"Yes. He keeps us informed of his whereabouts, he's very good in that way. I won't ask what you want to see him about, it's none of my business. However..." He paused to consult his watch. "He said he'd be at the Dane John around about twelve o'clock. I don't know why, he never said, but it's getting on for that now so if you go there you'll probably find him. I take it you know where it is?"

"Oh yes. Thank you." She recalled the old mound perfectly, the remains of a motte and bailey castle with ornamental gardens surrounding it. It was a spot she used to frequent at weekends, when she needed to get away from Botolph Street and the Berwicks. When she left the police station she made her way straight there. The route was automatic, something she didn't need to think about. Old habit took over.

The mound and the gardens around it hadn't changed when she got there. Or hardly changed, anyway. She had been half expecting, half fearing, bomb craters and destruction but the Dane John seemed to have escaped almost unscathed. The mound itself, with its winding hedged path to the top, was intact. The city walls still stood, solid as ever. The green area between was as peaceful as it had been in peacetime. People were wandering around, as they always did, enjoying the quiet, the semblance of normality. Eileen stood on a path between mound and walls and looked around her. Something was missing, something that had been there before. She frowned.

Of course, the bandstand. Over there between the walls and the mound there had been an ornate victorian bandstand, brightly painted. She'd always liked it, and now it had gone. She was sure of the site, knew precisely where it had been, and even now when she looked closely, there was a tell tale circular mark on the grass to show where it had been. There was no crater though, no evidence of any bomb damage. Just a blank empty space where there had once been a bandstand. It took a few moments before she drew the obvious conclusion. It had been made mostly of wrought iron, so would probably have been yet another victim of the voracious appetite for scrap metal, raw material for tanks and artillery. The enthusiasm for the war effort sometimes gave the impression of being no more than an excuse for vandalism. An unpatriotic thought, of course, but even so...

She found an empty bench along the path and sat down. She was suddenly very tired. The prolonged strain of her work, the train journey, the more or less constant activity since her arrival, the night disturbed by an air raid... these things had left her feeling exhausted. She had kept going, trying to ignore them and pretending they'd had no effect, but abruptly, in such peaceful surroundings and with no immediate need for action, the tiredness was free to take over. The day had grown warmer as it went on and now, near midday, the sun was hot. The heat seeped through the serge of the uniform and Eileen could feel her limbs relaxing under its influence. There could be no harm in sitting back for a while, sinking against the curved back of the bench, even closing her eyes for a few minutes...

She drifted. Her mind wandered. She didn't dream, exactly, but the quiet of the surroundings was suddenly filled by voices she knew, voices that came to her over the telephone, tinny and metallic, the familiar voices of radar operators, of Royal Observer Corps watchers.

Planes approaching the coast, about twenty of them, bearing one three zero, twelve thousand feet. Unidentified as yet.

Thirty or more, over Hastings and heading north west. Dorniers, possibly, with fighter escort. Flying at fifteen thousand feet.

Could they be trusted? Were they accurate? If so, what did they mean? Scramble the RAF fighters or not? If she didn't pass it on and it was a genuine raid, people would die. If she did and it turned out to be a decoy or just somebody's overactive imagination, the fighters would be unavailable in other places and people might still die.

Decisions, always decisions. Decisions made without enough time, without enough evidence, but they had to be made one way or the other nevertheless. Not making them was impossible. If you didn't make a decision and did nothing, that was in itself a decision.

I've got something here, but I can't tell what. It might be Lancasters from 106 squadron on their way home. On the other hand, it might not be... If it is, they're earlier than expected and there aren't many of them.

Dozens of them, and whatever they are I don't think they can be ours. Too many to count. They're coming in fast, heading north.

Decisions. Panic... No, there was no time to panic. Panic would be a disaster. Just decide.

Heinkels, they look like. Passing overhead now, can't see how many, there's too much cloud. Lots of the buggers, though. Sorry miss, pardon my greek.

Decisions.

Eileen twitched her head to dismiss the insistent voices and the abrupt movement jerked her out of her reverie. Her eyes blinked open and, disconcerted, she saw Ragley sitting on the bench beside her, smiling and smoking his inevitable pipe.

Chapter VII

"You were asleep. You looked very peaceful"

"I wasn't asleep, and whatever it looked like I certainly wasn't feeling peaceful. If you must know, I was thinking about work."

"Ah yes, work. I suppose it dominates the mind, it's bound to. All that shift work as well, it always throws you out of routine when you return to normal hours, doesn't it? No wonder you were feeling tired. But you should try to make the most of your leave." He drew on the pipe and blew out a little cloud of smoke. "And talking of making the most of it, I gather you wanted to see me."

"I did, yes." The reverie had gone, the voices temporarily stilled. The present had reimposed itself. "I've been talking to a neighbour from the next street. Baines, her name is, Charlotte Baines. Everybody calls her Lottie."

Ragley sat there, pipe in mouth, saying nothing.

"She told me David Berwick came home on leave during the war, and his friend Paul Chase was with him. He stayed in Botolph Street, the two of them were there together."

"Were they indeed? Well, there you are. I hadn't known that. You've earned your keep already. Not that it gets us any further forward, in a way. The body could still be either of them, couldn't it?" He sat there for a moment, puffing away with an air of placid contentment. Suddenly he said, irrelevantly, "Do you know what that is?" He was pointing with the stem of his pipe at two low doorways that had been built into the rampart beneath the city walls.

"What? No, I don't. Does it matter?"

"Not really. I just wondered, that's all."

Eileen studied the doors. They were quite modern. "An air raid shelter?" she guessed.

"You'd think so, wouldn't you? That would be sensible, under the circumstances. But it's not."

"No?" Eileen couldn't think of anything else to say.

"No. The thing is, it's an ammunition store. A bit silly, don't you think? I mean, I know it's pretty well protected down there but even so, a direct hit... It could blow the whole place up."

"Should you be telling me things like that?"

Ragley smiled. "Probably not. On the other hand, I expect everybody knows anyway. When I say everybody, I mean local people. They always know more than they're supposed to. But about David Berwick..." He looked down at his pipe, which appeared to have gone out. Without hurrying, he carefully relit it. "David Berwick. Yes, I've asked a few questions of various people. I know some people, you see, know who to ask... I know he went on home leave in 1916, that's on record. And I know he never came back. He just went home and never came back. He wasn't the only one of course. Once you got home, going back to the front wasn't a very appealing prospect. I remember it well. I could very easily have done the same myself."

"You were there?"

"At the front? Yes. Most men of my age were."

"But you obviously didn't desert."

"No. Well... call of duty and all that. You don't want to let people down, let your friends down. I'm sure you can understand that."

"Of course I can. But that's what David Berwick did?"

"Yes."

Eileen lit a cigarette and drew heavily on it. "His parents always said he'd died in the war."

"They would say that, wouldn't they?" He spoke mildly, without rancour. "Nobody wants to admit to a deserter in the family, a coward he would have been called then. That would be especially true of the Berwicks, from what I've learned of them. It would be a disgrace, a social humiliation. They wouldn't have wanted that. They'd have kept quiet about it. The Military Police would have come round asking questions, naturally, when David didn't show up after his leave had ended. But I'm sure they'd have found some way of accounting for that."

"Yes, I'm sure they would. But if it's true that David didn't go back after his leave...." She paused. "Does Inspector Jeffrey know that, by the way?"

"Not yet. He'll find out, eventually."

"You didn't think you ought to tell him?"

"Oh..." Ragley gazed down at the smouldering bowl of tobacco. "It's always more convincing if one finds out these things for oneself, don't you think? More satisfying, too."

"But doesn't it mean that the body is almost certainly David's?"

Ragley sat and thought for a moment. At last he said, "Almost, yes. Almost. You could say that. It wouldn't explain why he was wearing Paul Chase's identity bracelet, though. That's an oddity, isn't it?"

"Yes it is, but even so..." A thought suddenly occurred to Eileen. "You said it was Chase you were interested in. Do you know what happened to him when the leave was over?"

He beamed at her. "As a matter of fact, I do."

"I thought you might."

"Yes. He didn't return to his unit, but then he wasn't supposed to. He'd been transferred. He did go back though, to his new unit. That's all on record, too."

"Well if one of them went back and the other didn't..." Impatiently, Eileen stubbed out her cigarette.

"Then," Ragley went on unperturbed, "a few months later, Paul Chase was killed. Died in action, at Ypres. Like a lot of other men."

Eileen glared at him, increasingly irritated. "I don't understand this. The whole thing looks perfectly straightforward to me. I don't know exactly what happened in Botolph Street and I don't suppose I ever will, but nevertheless there were two men there, one of them is accounted for and the other isn't. What could be simpler? I suppose you are quite sure Paul Chase was killed?"

"It seems so." He looked sidelong at her. "His name's carved on the Menin Gate, as clearly as anyone else's. *Ad Majorem Dei Gloriam*, as the inscription says. To the greater glory of God. I've never been able to work out what it all has to do with the glory of God, but that's just a cynical old soldier talking. The thing is, Chase's name is there. I haven't seen it myself, travel to Ypres being rather hazardous these days, but I'm assured it's there."

"Then that settles it, doesn't it? It's all been a great fuss about nothing. I can't understand why you said you were so interested in Chase in the first place. I mean, if he's dead..." She paused suddenly. Ragley was looking at her, with that deceptively benign smile on his round face. "The Menin Gate?"

"Yes."

"But isn't that a memorial for the dead of Ypres with no known grave?"

He nodded. "It is."

"In which case," Eileen spoke slowly, thinking it out as she went along, "that means he was known to be killed because somebody found his body but couldn't recover it for burial. But they identified it..."

58

"...by his identity discs. Yes. That's how it worked. It still does."

"I see."

Ragley drew on his pipe and let out a plume of blue smoke. "It's all a question of identity, isn't it? Whose body was in the cellar of thirteen Botolph Street, whose body was found on the battlefield of Ypres? I do need to find out, you know."

"But you can't tell me why."

"I'm afraid not." He was apologetic. "I wish I could, but I'd probably be sacked if I did. Sacked, or worse."

Eileen thought about it. Absently she lit another cigarette even though she'd only just finished the last one. "Lottie said this man Chase who interests you so much was always talking about his home. Quite obsessed with it, apparently. You don't happen to know where he lived before the war, do you?"

"Oh yes. I've done my homework on the man. He was born and brought up on a farm not all that far from here. That's why he and David Berwick ended up in the same regiment, the local regiment, the Buffs. Why?"

"Just that if he was so attached to it, don't you think that if he was still alive he may have gone back there?"

Ragley appeared to ponder the suggestion. "No, I don't think so."

"Why not?"

"Well, for one thing it would be too obvious. If you were missing believed dead you wouldn't go home, would you? That's the first place anyone would look for you."

"And *have* you looked for him there?"

He looked uncomfortable. "As a matter of fact, no."

Eileen couldn't help but smile smugly. Ragley, for all his careful politeness could sometimes convey an irritating impression of quiet omniscience. "Overlooking the obvious, perhaps?"

"Perhaps," He admitted. "Do you think we should look there?"

"I think so. It was his home, he loved the place, apparently. People do tend to head for home when they're in trouble, don't they? It's an instinct of some sort."

Ragley thought about it. He took his pipe from his mouth and studied the bowl pointlessly. It was a habit she'd noticed before. Then he looked at her, one of those sideways looks she was getting used to. "Would *you* care to look there?"

"Me? Why?"

"Why not?" He didn't mention the extra week's leave, didn't even appeal to patriotism or duty; he just asked the question. He was, Eileen thought, an extraordinarily difficult man to deal with. He never said quite what you expected him to say.

"I suppose I could, if you wanted me to. Where is it, exactly? Do you know?"

"Oh yes. No problem there. I know just where it is, I've looked it up on a map." Suddenly, unexpectedly, he grinned. "It's in the middle of nowhere, that's where it is. Figuratively speaking, of course. It's a remote spot, miles from the nearest railway station. I shouldn't imagine there are many buses go that way either. If you were to go there you'd need transport. Do you drive?"

"No." Eileen didn't elaborate. Her training had included some driving lessons in RAF lorries, but she preferred to forget her performance in that particular area. It had been an embarrassing and potentially dangerous experience.

"Ah... That's a pity. It would have been convenient if you could. Never mind, I dare say I'll be able to arrange something." He consulted his watch. "There's really no need to do anything today, I'm sure you could do with a rest, and somewhere rather more comfortable than a park bench. How about if I send a car with a driver round tomorrow morning, after breakfast?"

Eileen laughed. "I was about to ask whether you could really do that, but I won't bother. You seem to be able to do anything you want."

"Oh, hardly that. But there are always ways and means, you know."

"I don't know, but I'll believe you." She stood up. "So I've the rest of the day to myself?"

"Of course. Enjoy your leave." Was that a subtle reminder that she owed the length of her leave directly to him? If so, it wasn't obvious from his expression or tone of voice.

"I will. Thank you." She turned to leave then abruptly turned back. "I was wondering..."

"Yes?" he encouraged her.

"What brought you here? I don't mean Canterbury, I know about that. I mean what brought you to this particular spot at this time of day? What made you decide on the Dane John?"

Ragley smiled placidly. "Nothing, really. I just thought it would be a pleasant, peaceful place to eat my lunch." He patted his gas mask case. "Sandwiches, you know."

"You've been here before, then?"

"Yes. A long time ago, though." He looked around. "It hasn't changed much, despite the war and the bombing and everything. It's still a peaceful spot. I seem to remember there used to be a bandstand somewhere, a big wrought iron thing. Over there, wasn't it?"

"Yes, that's right."

"I wonder what happened to it?" he mused. "Salvage, I expect. That's a pity, I used to like it. They call it salvage, but sometimes it seems to amount almost to vandalism. Ripping up a thing like that... I'm sure the

61

value of the iron to the war effort isn't really worth it." He looked at her. "You seem disconcerted. I hope you're not offended by my lack of patriotic fervour."

"No, not at all. I was just surprised because as a matter of fact exactly the same thought occurred to me just before you arrived."

"Did it?" He seemed amused. "A case of great minds thinking alike, perhaps."

Chapter VIII

After her meeting with Ragley, Eileen had very little to occupy her for the rest of the day. It was just spare time, and lately she hadn't had much practice in filling spare time. There hadn't been enough of it to make filling it a problem.

She lingered over a small lunch in a town centre café. It was a genteel sort of establishment, which was incongruous considering the bomb sites on either side of it, and the lunch was small because she wasn't used to large meals these days. The food provided at Rudloe Manor was basic, and you weren't given much time to eat it before you were expected back on duty. Time spent sitting at a table, complete with elaborate and spotlessly clean lace tablecloth, was luxury indeed. Afterwards, she sat back in her chair with a pot of tea and a delicate china cup and saucer in front of her, and slowly smoked two cigarettes. It was odd; her table was next to a window and the buildings on the other side of the road were untouched, the ruins on either side of the café invisible. Everything looked and felt deceptively normal.

The question was, what to do with the rest of the day?

There were a few things she needed from the shops. She had brought only enough with her for her original forty eight hour leave; a week was a different matter. Most essentials were provided by the hotel, but not all. So... a little shopping, but that wouldn't take long. After that? She stubbed out the second cigarette in the brass ash tray provided and stood up. After that, she'd see when the time came.

There was no one she really wanted to look up, no old friends or anything like that. Canterbury had never really been her home, it had just been somewhere she had stayed for a while. There was nowhere she particularly wanted to go; she had already visited the cathedral and the Dane John, had viewed the remains of thirteen Botolph Street. That was about it. What she finally decided to do, with her little shopping over, was to return to her hotel and rest for a while. There was no harm in that, after all. Just a little lie down, after which she would think again. She was weary, fagged out.

Ragley had been right, she thought, about the shift work. When you came off it you were fine at first, relieved to be back to normal. But that was an illusion, you weren't normal. It took a couple of days to catch up with you but when it did it left you tired, worn out. Your mind and body needed time to adapt to the different patterns expected of them. In between, you became tired at unexpected times and wide awake at others. It could be very inconvenient.

In her room at the hotel she lay on the bed, not bothering to undress for such a brief nap, and closed her eyes...

When she opened them again and looked at the clock she was bewildered for a moment, thought at first she must be making some ridiculous mistake like a child misreading the position of the hands on the dial. But no... She picked up the clock and stared at it in disbelief. She had been asleep for more than four hours and it would soon be time for the evening meal. That came as a shock. She sat up on the edge of the bed, feeling irrationally guilty as if she'd missed the start of a shift, or been sleeping on duty.

But you're not on duty, she told herself irritably,

you're on leave. You're perfectly entitled to sleep as much as you want.

She poured water from the jug into the enamel bowl, splashed her face then vigorously towelled it dry. The cold water and rough towel would wake her up, if they did nothing else.

The odd thing was that she didn't recall being affected quite so much in the past. There had always been a little readjustment required, but it had never been of any significance. She had taken it in her stride, as she did so many other things. On the other hand, it had been quite a long time since she'd had any leave. Perhaps her memory was playing tricks...

No.

No, it wasn't that, she was sure of it. Perhaps it was just that she was getting older. She glared at the mirror above the bowl, resenting as usual the woman who glared back at her. Even so, she wasn't *old*. Nobody would describe twenty four as *old*, would they? She was, however, the oldest woman in the filter room. There was no getting away from that. She hadn't been allowed to forget the fact; there had been quite a few tiresomely juvenile jokes about it. Most of the girls there were at least four years younger than her, some of them more than that; hardly more than schoolgirls really, and one or two had a sense of humour to match. Not that any of them were completely open about it, not when their target was a sergeant, but nevertheless Eileen was well aware of the comments that had been made, as she had been intended to be.

Oh well, forget it. She was tired. That was all it came down to, regardless of the reason. She wouldn't sleep well tonight though, not after passing out for four hours in the afternoon. She wondered about taking another walk around the town but the idea didn't appeal. In the end she just took out the boring detective story she'd brought with her and lay down with it until dinner time. She couldn't work out whodunnit, mostly because she couldn't work up any interest in any of the characters (including the corpse), but it would pass the time as well as anything else.

Chapter IX

The following morning, as usual, she started off by going to the reception desk and asking for messages. The old man shook his head slowly.

"No messages today, no."

"Thank you." Eileen turned to leave.

"But..."

The man was really infuriating. "Yes?"

He nodded towards the front door. "There's somebody waiting for you outside. She asked me to tell you she was here."

She? "Well she can wait until I've had breakfast. I'm hungry. If she comes in again, whoever she is, tell her she can carry on waiting."

"I'll tell her." He sounded as if he might gain some satisfaction from relaying the message.

Eileen sat down to breakfast. Despite her misgivings, she had actually slept quite well and felt better for it. Her table was next to a window and if she looked out she could see the street. There was a car parked there, an old Austin Eight, probably pre-war, black and rather the worse for wear. A WAAF aircraftswoman was leaning up against it, smoking a cigarette and looking bored. The driver, presumably. Eileen watched her with disapproval. She had a casual, rather scruffy look about her. Not a good advertisement for the service, not smart enough by a long chalk. Her make up was ostentatious, her cap at far too rakish an angle, her hair covering the top of the uniform collar, and... yes, you could see when she turned round, she was wearing her stockings inside out. That was one of the oldest tricks in the book. The stockings were thick and if you turned them inside out it made the seams stand out. A lot of them did that, thought it made their legs look better.

If she's the one waiting for me, Eileen thought, we'll have words before we part.

She didn't hurry her breakfast, and lingered afterwards over a pot of tea and two cigarettes. Eventually though, she went out. The driver saw her, hurriedly dropped the cigarette she was smoking and stepped on it. Then, as an afterthought, she stood to attention and saluted.

"You must be new. I'm a sergeant, you don't salute me. You only salute officers."

"Yes sergeant. Sorry, sergeant. I did know that only... well, I forgot."

"Don't forget again. What's your name, aircraftswoman?"

"Dowding, sergeant."

Eileen stared at her. "Dowding? Is that supposed to be a joke of some sort?"

"No, sergeant. It's just my name, that's all. No relation, as far as I know. There have been a few jokes about it."

"I'll bet there have. Never mind, let's make a start." Eileen climbed into the back of the car, Dowding into the driver's seat. "Do you know where we're going?"

"Yes, sergeant."

"Then you're one up on me. Where is it?"

"Longmeadow farm." If Dowding found it odd her passenger didn't know the destination, she betrayed no sign of it. "It's not far. I've got the map coordinates and I've looked it up. It shouldn't take more than half an hour or so."

"Good. Don't get lost."

"I won't." The old Austin drew out into the road and travelled slowly through the town, finally leaving it by the old Dover road. Dowding proved to be a good, competent driver, unhurried, smooth through the gear changes, gentle on the brakes. Eileen found she could relax on the back seat. Dowding didn't say anything unless directly invited to, which was also a pleasant change. Most drivers, in Eileen's experience, were compulsive talkers - like hairdressers or dentists.

The car rolled on along the old road, uneventful, unexciting.

"Do you know anything about this farm?"

"Nothing, sergeant, except for its position on the map. It looks like a pretty isolated spot. There's nothing else marked for miles."

The Kent Downs passed by, rural and quiet. Fields and trees, the occasional cluster of houses, nothing else. Eventually, the car took a side road, narrow and winding with thick old hedges on either side. Dowding manoeuvred competently, taking the bends slowly and making full use of the gearbox. Eventually, after about the predicted half hour, she brought the car to a halt. They were opposite a narrow track that led off to the right.

"It's down there, I think. There's no sign, but I'm sure that must be it. It's the only turn off I've seen. I can take the car down there if you like, sergeant, but I'm not sure the suspension would be up to it."

"How far is it?"

"On the map it looks like a couple of hundred yards, no more than that."

"I'll walk it from here, then. There's no point in breaking air force equipment for the sake of two hundred yards." She got out of the car and slammed the door behind her. It was the sort of door that needed to be slammed.

"Would you like me to wait here for you, sergeant?"

"No. I don't know how long I'll be." The day was warm and the driver's window was fully open. Eileen bent down and poked her head in. "Come back and pick me up in... Oh, I don't know." She looked at her watch. "Let's say two hours."

"Very well, sergeant."

"Oh, and before you go... You're a good driver, Dowding."

"Thank you, sergeant. I usually drive lorries. This is child's play by comparison."

"I'm sure. Anyway, credit where it's due, you're a good driver. In other ways, though, there's room for improvement. Before I see you again, make sure your cap's straight, tuck your hair up so that it doesn't touch your collar, and put your stockings on as they're meant to be. Got that?"

"Yes, sergeant. Sorry, sergeant."

"And next time you're out in public, exercise a bit of restraint with the cosmetics. You're an aircraftswoman, remember - not a walking advertisement for Max Factor. Still... you're a good driver. Be here in two hours." Eileen tapped the roof of the car in dismissal and started off along the farm track. Behind her, she heard the car turn and start back along the road. There was no unnecessary revving of the engine or screech of tyres to indicate anger. Yes, Dowding was a good and conscientious driver.

The track was narrow and rough, and the dry weather had hardened the ruts so that it was like walking over uneven corrugated iron. You had to watch where you stepped or risk a turned ankle.

Even so, under a clear blue sky, it was a pleasant walk. For once, the war hardly seemed to exist. There was no drone of aircraft engines overhead, no threat of bombs. Everything was calm and green and peaceful. The sun was warm, as it had been for several days; warm, and becoming hot as the day progressed. By the afternoon, Eileen thought, the uniform was going to start becoming uncomfortable. She walked on, more slowly than was customary with her, taking her time and enjoying the surroundings. Something about the hedges and trees on either side of the track was quintessentially English, the old nostalgic dream of a rural England that had perhaps never really existed but remained nevertheless a powerful presence. Chaucer's pilgrims, she reflected, would have recognised tracks like this. Although the practical part of her, never far below the surface, observed that they would have been further north. Still, that wouldn't have made much difference. The countryside would have been much the same.

There was no one about, she had the track to herself. The quiet was almost absolute, her own footsteps the only sound other than birdsong. The shrill, impatient calls of blackbirds and the constant cawing of rooks were so appropriate a background noise they hardly intruded at all. They were a part of the scene, an audible equivalent to the trees and the hedgerows.

The walk, short though it was if measured out, seemed to take an inordinately long time. As always, an unfamiliar route seems long the first time you take it. Eventually though, she reached what must surely be Longmeadow farm. The track ended at a pair of wooden five bar gates, old and in a state of poor repair. Beyond the gates lay a rough, overgrown yard. Chickens wandered about, pecking randomly at the ground. There was a house, brick built and not particularly large, and scattered around it to no obvious plan, a motley collection of sheds, small barns and wooden structures whose purpose it was impossible to determine. Somewhere out of sight a cow lowed mournfully. It was all very traditional. Eileen felt a sudden, ridiculous pang of nostalgia for a world and a way of life she had never known and probably wouldn't have liked anyway. Even so, this was England, home and beauty. This was what they were all fighting for. A ridiculous idea, of course. There were probably similar farms all over Bavaria and Saxony.

She lifted the latch of the gates and stepped through, carefully closing the gates behind her. She would go straight to the house and knock on the front door. There was no one else about, so it was the only thing she could do. She wondered what she would say, how she would introduce herself. She hadn't given the matter any thought. She'd think of something when the time came.

As she approached the house, however, someone emerged from one of the barns. It was a woman - or more of a girl really, still in her teens. She was wearing a Women's Land Army uniform of green jumper, breeches, long socks and heavy brown shoes. She was a little slip of a thing, short and thin with blonde hair tied back. She was also very grubby and was pushing a wheelbarrow whose contents looked heavier than she was. Barn manure, at a guess. It looked like it and smelled like it. When she saw Eileen she dropped the handles of the barrow and walked round it.

"Hello. Are you lost?" The voice was pleasant, quiet, educated. Unexpected.

"No, I don't think so. This is Longmeadow farm, isn't it?"

"Yes, that's right. But we don't get many visitors. Usually the only time anyone ends up here is if they're lost. Can I help you?"

Eileen looked at the house. "Well, I was just going to..."

"There's no point knocking on the door, there's nobody in. They're out in the fields. It's that time of year, you know. Mind you, they say that at nearly any time of year. You know what farmers are like."

"Actually, no I don't."

"That's all right. Neither did I until I came here. It's been a bit of an eye-opener, I can tell you." She pulled a packet of cigarettes from the pocket of her breeches, lit it and offered the pack to Eileen. "Here, want one?"

"Thanks." Eileen took it and accepted the offer of a light. "My name's Eileen, by the way."

"Pleased to meet you. Alice." She held up her hands, caked with something unmentionable and very brown. "I won't offer to shake hands."

"No." Eileen grinned. "I'd probably have to turn down the offer. Anyway, I'm not lost. I'm here here looking for someone called Chase. The Chase family do still own this farm, don't they?"

"No. I've never heard of them. But then again I'm not local, as you may have guessed from the accent. They may have been here at some time, but if they were they're gone now."

"I did guess you weren't local. As you say, the accent's a give away. So what are you doing here?"

"Isn't that obvious? Women's Land Army. You don't think I wear these clothes by choice, do you? Credit me with more taste than that, please. I was the right age for call up, so I thought I'd join something or other while I still had the choice. I didn't fancy what you've done, all that parade ground stuff and saluting and so on, so it was either the WLA or a munitions factory." She paused to draw on the cigarette. "Have you ever been inside a munitions factory?"

"No," Eileen confessed.

"I have. They're awful places. Besides, in the nature of things they're prime targets for the Luftwaffe. No, I decided in the end I'd be better off in the middle of a field somewhere. Fresh air and less chance of being bombed. Anyway, I'm straying from the point. You were asking after somebody. I can't help you, but I know somebody who might." She shouted over her shoulder, back towards the barn. "Maggie! Come out, there's somebody to talk to you. Maggie's local," she added more quietly. "You'll know that as soon as she opens her mouth. She's been around here all her life. If there was ever a Chase family in these parts, she'll know about it even if it goes back to the Domesday book."

Another girl in WLA uniform appeared out of the bar, a fork slung over her shoulder. She was about the same age as Alice, but in every other respect was an exact opposite. She was tall, heavy, bulky, with the ruddy complexion of someone who spends most of her time outdoors. When she walked forward and the two of them stood next to one another, Eileen was irresistibly reminded of a young female version of Laurel and Hardy. It was difficult not to laugh at the contrast.

"This is Eileen, Maggie."

Maggie nodded. "Pleased to meet you. Don't know what you're doing here, though. Nobody ever comes here." Yes, the voice was unmistakably local.

"I've already told her that. She's looking for some people called Chase. Have you ever heard of them?"

"Oh yes, I've heard of them. They used to live here. Owned the farm, they did, or so I was told, but that was before my time. You won't find anybody of that name around here now." She shifted the fork from her shoulder and thrust it into the ground with one hand and an apparent lack of effort.

"That's a pity. It looks as if my information was quite a bit out of date. They sold the farm, did they?"

"No. They died."

"And there was nobody to inherit? That's a shame."

Maggie shrugged. "It happens."

"I was told there was a son. That's who I'm looking for, as a matter of fact. You don't happen to know..."

"He's dead too. Killed in the war; the last war, that is, not this one. There'd been some sort of family trouble, or so my mother told me. He wasn't welcome at the farm any more. Not that it makes much difference if they're all dead, does it?"

"I suppose not. Look, I'm sorry if I'm being a bit vague but I can't help it. This man Chase would be in his forties now. I'm looking for man of about that age..."

Alice giggled. "Aren't we all? Especially if he happens to be rich. But there aren't many men living close to here, worse luck, and I don't think any of them are that age. There's nobody, I'm afraid."

"Yes there is." Maggie was firm. "There's old scarface, down at the cottage."

"Maggie, you're awful! You shouldn't call him that."

"Why not? He's got a scar on his face, hasn't he?"

"Yes, but..."

"There you are then. Anyway, he can't hear me from here, can he? If he can't hear me, it's not going to bother him."

"Even so..." But Alice clearly gave up a lost cause. "But besides anything else, he's not the right age. He's older than that."

"No he isn't. He just looks older because of the scar.

Alice was doubtful. "Are you sure?"

"Yes."

The comparison with Laurel and Hardy was growing more convincing all the time. "Perhaps I'd better talk to him, just to see. Where can I find him?"

"At the cottage." Maggie wasn't particularly helpful.

"Don't be silly. Eileen won't know where that is, will she? Look, if you go back out of the gate you'll see a path leading into the trees off to your left. At the end of it there's what used to be an old gamekeeper's cottage, it's not far. He lives there. His real name's Copper, by the way, and he doesn't work for the farm he just rents the place. He's got a business of his own of some sort, I don't really know what, but it does take him away quite often, whatever it is, so he may not be there."

"I'll take a chance," said Eileen. "Thanks for your help."

"Any time."

The path into the trees turned out to be quite obvious. The track she'd walked along ended at the farm gate and the farm itself was quite low lying with wooded slopes on three sides. The trees didn't seem to extend to any great distance as far as she could see, but there was only one discernible way through them, a little path no more than three or four foot wide and encroached upon on either side by ferns, nettles and cleavers. Eileen strode out along it. It was clearly frequently used because despite the invasive undergrowth the path itself was quite clear and firm.

It was darker and cool under the trees, with the slight but pervasive smell of damp you always get in woodland. The warmth of June was gradually increasing with the approach of midday; warm was quickly intensifying into uncomfortably hot. The shade of the trees, which at other times may have seemed rather oppressive, was at that time of day quite welcome. The path was, as Alice had promised, quite short, though it was also mostly uphill. At the end of it Eileen came to a clearing in the trees. In front of her was the old gamekeeper's cottage. It couldn't possibly be anything else.

It was an odd little place, with something of the brothers Grimm about it. The building itself was ramshackle, paint peeling from door and windows, moss growing thick on the roof. The structure was brick but had at some time been limewashed, a coating that was now visible only as uneven patchy stains and was no longer white but had taken on a pale green tint as if it had been infected by the surrounding trees. There was no garden as such, and no fence. There was only a roughly cleared area which was bare except for clumps of thick, coarse grass and the usual detritus of human habitation; buckets and tools left lying about, many of them rusty, some damaged; a couple of old chairs that had obviously been thrown out and left to rot outside.

It was untidy, yes - untidy and neglected. But more than that, there was something vaguely unsettling about it, something that made one a little uneasy. It certainly wasn't at all welcoming or homely. And it was absolutely silent. There was no sound of animal or bird life, though there surely must be birds in these trees and small animals hiding beneath them. Perhaps her own arrival had silenced them, made them wary. But in a rural, isolated spot like this you would expect something like the more domestic noise of chickens, or a dog barking to warn of intruders. There was nothing.

"Quiet, isn't it?" The voice, coming apparently out of nowhere, startled her and she jumped. Then, annoyed by the nervousness her own reaction betrayed, she looked around. A man had appeared round the corner of the cottage and was leaning against the wall. He must have moved very slowly and quietly for his arrival not to have attracted her attention.

"Yes. Very quiet."

"I like it like that. It wouldn't suit most people, but it suits me." He pushed himself away from the wall and started to walk slowly towards her. "I don't get many visitors. What brings you here, sergeant?"

As he drew closer, she studied his appearance. He was a solid, muscular man dressed in baggy corduroy

77

trousers held up by a wide leather belt, an open necked woollen shirt and a plain neckerchief. His feet were encased by a pair of heavy and well-worn leather boots. The traditional rustic labourer, as if he had dressed specially for the part in some theatrical production. The hair was roughly cut, uncombed and probably unwashed, starting to show signs of grey around the temples. He was, she thought, almost too much of a stereotype to be true. Age? Yes, he could easily be in his forties. The face could have been quite presentable, handsome even, if not for the scar. It was an old dry scar, running down the left side of his face from the corner of the eye as far as the chin. The tanned skin of an outdoor life made it stand out even more than it would have done, livid and white. It must have been a nasty wound when he got it, though that had obviously happened a long time ago. The skin was puckered around it, distorting the otherwise regular features and making him look somehow lopsided. Old scarface, as Maggie had called him, and it was true that the scar did dominate his appearance; you couldn't even pretend not to notice it.

"I'm looking for someone."

"Well, there's only me here. Was it me you were looking for?"

"I don't know."

He grinned. The grin was natural enough and perfectly amiable, but the stiff scar tissue twisted it into something slightly sinister. "If you don't know who you're looking for, how will you know when you find him? That's silly, that is."

"I know his name, I just don't know what he looks like. His name's Chase, Paul Chase."

"Well my name's Copper, so you haven't found who you're looking for. I've never heard of anybody called Chase."

"I'd have thought you'd have been familiar with the name. His family used to own the farm. That's why I thought I might find him here. People tend to stick close to home, don't they? Especially country people."

"I haven't been here all that long. I don't know who owned the farm before I came, and I don't care much. I live in the present, sergeant, not in the past." He didn't seem eager to be rid of her, seemed quite content to stand and talk. Perhaps he was just glad of some company. Or perhaps he was another one of those men who were attracted by women in uniform. But no, she couldn't really believe that. He just wasn't the type, didn't look at her in that way at all.

"Talking of living in the present, how do you manage to make a living around here? You're not a farm worker, are you?"

"Me? No. I'm..." he hesitated. "I'm a mechanic of sorts. Farm machinery. I repair farm machinery."

"Ah. A reserved occupation, I expect. That explains why you're not in uniform. You would be eligible for conscription otherwise, wouldn't you? I mean, you're not too old."

Copper laughed. "No, I'm not too old. I sometimes feel it and I know I look it, but I'm not."

Eileen looked around at the trees and the narrow path. "Farm machinery? But nobody would be able to get a tractor up here, would they, let alone anything bigger?"

"No, they wouldn't. My customers don't come to me, they write telling me there's a job to do, and I go to them. The post's delivered to the farm and I pick it up every day. I travel around a lot, all over the place. You could say I'm an itinerant worker; peripatetic, they call it. I've got a bike, you see."

"A bike?" Eileen was incredulous. "How far could you get on a bike, for heaven's sake? And how could you

79

carry any tools or spare parts? I don't believe it."

"Ah, but it's not just any old bike. Come and take a look, if you like." He turned and walked around the side of the cottage, apparently taking it for granted she would follow him - and after a moment's hesitation, she did. Despite the scar and the rough clothes, there was somehow nothing even remotely threatening about him.

There was a lean-to structure at the side of the cottage, made of rough wooden planking with a corrugated iron roof. Copper led her to it and opened the door.

"See?" Inside there was indeed a bicycle, protected from the elements. It was a strange looking thing, with what looked like a petrol engine bolted onto the bottom of the frame. Copper squatted down next to it and ran his hands over the frame, almost affectionately, the way you'd stroke a dog. "It's a Norman."

"Yes, I know."

He turned to look at her over his shoulder, appearing surprised. "You know? You know about machines, then?"

"No. It's just that it has the word 'Norman' printed on the petrol tank."

He laughed. "So it does. Well they're good machines, Normans. Made locally too, at the factory in Ashford, so I don't have any trouble getting hold of parts." He patted the engine beneath the tank. "It's a 98 cc Villiers. As good as you can get. Do you know, I can get thirty or more miles per hour out of this, on the flat."

"Can you?" Eileen tried to sound interested.

"I can. The suspension's good, too." He ran his hand down the front forks, which looked unusually thick and sturdy. "I have to travel on a lot of rough ground, going to farms as I do, so you need good suspension. These are single-spring Webb forks, they'll take you over almost anything providing you're careful. You wouldn't get better on a proper motorbike."

"Really? How interesting."

He laughed and pushed himself to his feet. He had to keep his head bowed to keep it below the level of the sloping roof. "All right, you're not interested. But it's my living, you know. And you did ask what I did for a living so you've only yourself to blame if you're bored."

"So I have, I admit it." Eileen left the shed, Copper following her and carefully closing the door behind him. They walked around to the front of the building where Eileen paused and turned back to him. "But you've never heard of Paul Chase? You're sure of that?"

"Perfectly sure. I hope you find him, whoever he is. You didn't say why you were looking for him, by the way?" He made it an implicit question.

"No. Well... it's a long story. He's supposed to be dead, you see."

"But you obviously don't think he is."

"No."

"When is he supposed to have died?"

It was a dilemma knowing how much to say, how much to conceal. "That's a more difficult question than it sounds, as well. You see, he seems to have died twice; once at Ypres during the last war, then again in Canterbury."

"Twice dead, but you still believe he's around somewhere?" He sounded amused. "The chap must have more lives than a cat."

"Yes, it does sound odd, doesn't it?"

They were in front of the cottage now, near the path that had brought her there. The silence, she noticed, had gone now. Everything was more normal. It must, after all, have been her arrival that had caused it. Birds were singing and there was a movement in the undergrowth beneath the trees. As she watched the nettles stirred and an animal crept out. At first she thought it may be a fox, but surprisingly it turned out to be a dog.

"Is that your dog?"

"No. I don't keep dogs. I've no need for them and they're more trouble than they're worth." Copper stooped to pick up a stone and threw it towards the dog, not aggressively but just to scare the animal off. The stone fell well short and The dog watched it land without moving, then casually wandered off back into the trees.

"It's funny, you know, but I could swear I've seen that dog before."

"It's just a mongrel, like a lot of others. Probably a local farm dog or a stray."

"But I saw it a long way away. In Canterbury."

Copper shrugged, apparently uninterested. "Dogs can roam quite a distance, especially strays. Besides, it's probably a different dog entirely."

"Probably."

But it wasn't. She was certain of it.

Chapter X

It was odd.

There was something decidedly odd about the whole thing.

Eileen stood by the side of the road, waiting for Dowding to return. She was a little early and had no doubt that her driver would turn up exactly on time, with military precision, if only to avoid being told off again. She consulted her watch: ten minutes yet. Dowding was probably sitting in the car a couple of hundred yards away with the engine running, consulting her own watch and waiting, just as Eileen was. It was all a bit silly when you thought about it. But that was the military for you, with all its faults and its virtues.

It was Copper that was odd. Well, the whole thing was odd including the dilapidated cottage in the woods, the motorised bicycle and the dog. But above all it was Copper himself. That scar of his that dominated his appearance but, in the name of politeness, was never mentioned. The fact that he had accepted her arrival, had hardly asked any questions. Surely, anyone would have been more curious than that; would have asked, for example, just *why* she was looking for Paul Chase; would have asked why she thought he (Copper) might be the man. He'd hardly seemed curious at all, had simply accepted everything. And that life of his, solitary and reclusive but combined with travel for work... Not many people would want to live like that.

Did that matter? People were entitled to live as they pleased. The fact that it was unusual was neither here nor there. It was a free country - at least, she made the mental qualification, at the moment it was.

Eileen glanced at her watch again. Still seven minutes to go.

Paul Chase, Lottie had told her, talked about nothing but his home and his dogs. Copper had said he didn't keep dogs, they were more trouble than they were worth, had casually thrown a stone at the dog when it appeared. Yet he lived very close to what had been the Chase farm. She was undecided. What she'd tell Ragley when he asked, as he inevitably would, she just didn't know.

The car arrived precisely two minutes early, obviously carefully timed. Eileen climbed into the back seat and, during the journey to Canterbury, stared at the back of Dowding's head. The cap was on straight and the hair had been tucked up neatly under it. So far so good. Whether anything had been done about the make-up and the stockings, she couldn't tell. Probably not. Those were rather more tricky to remedy in public. Still, her point had been made and the message acted upon. Dowding's driving was as competent as ever, smooth gear changes and gentle use of the brakes. All told, quite successful. Military discipline in action.

But it didn't help with what she would say to Ragley. It had been her own idea to go to Chase's old home, based partly on what Lottie had told her, and she felt some responsibility for the time and effort that had been expended. It would help if she could think of something positive to report.

What she actually said, when Ragley turned up at the hotel that afternoon, was "I don't know".

"You don't know?" He sat in the same chair of the residents' lounge, his attention seemingly taken up with the ritual of cleaning out his pipe and depositing the residue into the ash tray. "What don't you know, exactly?"

"Exactly, I don't know whether the man I met could be Paul Chase or not. He's the right sort of age and he's in the right place, but... It would help if we had a photograph of Paul Chase."

"It would indeed. I couldn't agree more." Ragley knocked out the pipe and proceeded to refill it from his leather pouch. The pouch looked as old and grubby as the pipe. "Unfortunately we don't have any photographs, not even very old ones. He's a mystery man, is our Mr Chase. You say this man you met had a scar on his face?"

"Yes. A very noticeable one."

"Hm... We don't have any record of that. But it could have happened at any time."

"Not recently."

"Not recently, no." Ragley gently and delicately tamped down the tobacco with his forefinger and put the pipe down to get out his matches. "Perhaps it would help things along if I told you just why we're so interested in Paul Chase."

"I should think it would, but that's something you said you weren't allowed to tell me."

"I did say that, didn't I? You're quite right." He struck a match and applied it to the tobacco, carefully moving it over the pipe bowl to ensure an even light. He seemed to be engrossed, paying her no attention at all. "However, one must use one's discretion. What's allowed and what's not allowed... well, that changes with circumstances, don't you think?"

"Are you sure your superiors would agree with you?"

He puffed out a cloud of smoke, shook the match out and suddenly grinned at her. "I'm not at all sure, since you ask. But they're not here and we are. Now, Paul Chase... where shall I start?" He looked around, apparently casually. Eileen followed his example, but there was no one in sight except for the old man in reception who was

85

paying them no attention at all and was too far away to hear anything if they spoke quietly. And Ragley, she'd noticed, always spoke quietly.

"The thing is, as I'm sure you know, that just as the Germans have people over here helping them - the notorious fifth column the newspapers keep talking about - in the same way we have people over there helping us."

"Spies, you mean?"

"Gracious me, no!" He sounded quite shocked. "Spies are nasty, underhand types, quite beyond the pale. No, we don't have spies, we have agents. Unlike spies, agents are heroic decent chaps. We have agents and the enemy has spies." He kept a straight face as he said it.

"I see."

"Good. Now, one of our agents - not a spy, mind you, an agent - one of our agents has access to information about their spies. Are you following me?"

"I'm having some trouble with the terminology, but yes. Go on."

"In short, he tells us who they are. The ones he knows about, that is. He doesn't know everything, not by a long way. He's not that high up in the hierarchy. Nevertheless, he's a useful and generally reliable source of information and he gave us the name of Paul Chase."

"I see."

"Yes. Don't repeat any of this by the way," he sounded suddenly anxious, "if anyone knew I'd told you..."

"Naturally not. Did you think I would?"

"No. If I'd thought that I wouldn't have told you in the first place. But the thing is, we had the name of a man who was supposed to be a German spy - yet when we checked up on him we discovered he was dead, died in the last war in Ypres. That was a bit of a puzzle. But after that a body was discovered in Canterbury with an identity bracelet. Well... we didn't quite know what to think. That was how I came to be here. We had to find out, you see; make sure we knew exactly where we were."

"You still don't though, do you?"

"Not yet," he admitted ruefully.

"Couldn't you just pick Copper up as a suspect and question him the way the police do?"

"I suppose we could, but it wouldn't help much. You see, even if he is a spy that's not really what we're after. Spies - real spies, I mean - don't work the way they do in fiction. They're not solitary creatures equipped with radios. They're part of a network, an organisation. If Copper is Chase, he'll have someone he passes his information on to. Several other spies will do the same. Then it's all sifted and collated - a bit like a filter room, if you'll forgive the comparison - and sent to Germany from a central source. It's that source we want. That would put the entire organisation out of action. Picking up one individual wouldn't really achieve very much in the long run."

"But wouldn't it be better than nothing?"

"Yes, in a way. In another way, it would be worse. It would just alert all the others and make it harder for us to nail them. You know..." he paused and stared down at his pipe. "One thing that interests me is that motorised bike you said he had. The Norman."

"That? It was the only thing he seemed genuinely interested in. Why is it that men get so emotional over machines? I've never understood it."

"Me neither." He smiled at her. "It's no good asking me, I'm afraid. I've never been any good with mechanical things. If I so much as look at a machine it breaks down. I sometimes think the best way I could serve my country would be to get a job in a German armaments factory. The whole place would be closed down within a week."

Eileen laughed despite herself. She couldn't help it, he looked so bland and innocent as he said it. "So why does Copper's bike interest you so much?"

"I used to know someone who had a Norman. He swore by it just the way Copper does, couldn't stop talking about it."

"He sounds utterly boring."

"He was. However, some of the things he said may be relevant. I can remember them. I ought to be able to, I heard them often enough. Besides all the stuff you heard from Copper about speed and so on, he used to say it was the perfect machine for an age of petrol rationing. He used to boast he could get 150 miles per gallon on a tank of petrol. That's quite a lot, isn't it? Most impressive." He paused and waited for a response.

"Most." Eileen thought about it, wondering what he was getting at. Then suddenly she realised. "Yes. That would put almost all of the channel ports within range, wouldn't it? And at thirty miles per hour, he could get to any of them and back within a day easily. And not only the ports... Biggin Hill as well, and..."

Ragley was nodding. "Exactly. Lots of places, very sensitive places. You see my point. And because his work takes him all over the place, nobody would question it. It's a perfect arrangement. I'll tell you something else as well."

"Go on," Eileen prodded.

"We know, of course, that David Berwick went missing after his leave and that Paul Chase returned. But he didn't return to his old unit in the Buffs. He'd been transferred." He paused for effect.

"Don't tease. Transferred to?"

"To the Royal Engineers. It's in his military record. He was put onto the maintenance of army transport vehicles and machinery. That's interesting, isn't it?"

"Under the circumstances, very interesting. Why didn't you tell me that before?"

"I wasn't to know that it would be relevant, was I? Besides, there's 'need to know' and all that. You didn't need to know, at the time. It may even have prejudiced your impressions. I'm telling you now, even though strictly speaking I shouldn't."

Absently, Eileen lit a cigarette. "So he would have had some training in the repair of machinery, and some interest in machinery. It's starting to come together, isn't it?"

"Don't jump to conclusions," he warned her. "There's still a lot we don't know."

"I'm not. All I was thinking is that perhaps I should pay another visit to Mr Copper and this time push a bit harder, see whether I can make him say something more definite - something that can be checked."

Ragley nodded. "If you want to. I'll leave it up to you. It certainly may help. You can have the use of the car again tomorrow if you want it, I've already arranged that."

Eileen raised her eyebrows. "Have you, indeed? That was taking rather a lot for granted, wasn't it?"

"Look upon it as foresight. I was just catering for possibilities, that's all. If the car and driver weren't required, it wouldn't matter."

"The same driver?"

"Yes."

"That's good. Aircraftswoman Dowding was very competent."

It was Ragley's turn for the raised eyebrows. "Dowding? Was that really her name?"

"Yes. No relation, she assured me. Mind you, when I ticked her off about her hair and her stockings I still felt as if I were criticising an air chief marshal."

"Hair and stockings?"

"Don't ask."

"I won't," he assured her. "It sounds as though it may be slightly indelicate, in which case I'd rather not know."

"Rather not know? I thought you people always wanted to know everything. You're a funny sort of military intelligence officer, if you'll forgive me saying so."

Ragley put his pipe into his mouth and beamed amiably at her. "Aren't I just?"

Chapter XI

Eileen fell asleep again during the afternoon, but this time not for as long. She was adapting though not, she reflected, as quickly as she used to. Once awake she lay on the bed for a while, her limbs feeling heavy and reluctant to move, mentally going over her conversation with Ragley.

The original problem, she mused, had not gone away. It had become more complicated but it was still awkwardly, obstinately there. Whose body had been found in the ruins of thirteen Botolph Street? At one time she'd thought it had been resolved. David Berwick was missing, Paul Chase had died at Ypres; therefore, the body must be David's. But then things had moved on. Paul Chase hadn't died, according to Ragley's mysterious German source. And it was definitely true his death had only been established by his identity discs, and that may be no more reliable than the discs found on the body in Botolph Street. Someone had definitely died there, that was an indisputable fact but it didn't help.

If only there was a photograph somewhere, of either of them.

Would she honestly be able to identify Copper from a twenty six year old photograph? The years changed a man, sometimes beyond recognition. So did a prominent facial scar. Yet it wasn't impossible, though she recalled Lottie saying the two men had been physically very alike, which would of course make identification even more difficult.

Abruptly, she sat up on the bed.

Lottie. "Quite taken with me, he was, though I

shouldn't be the one to say it. At the time I thought... well, if there hadn't been the war we might have..." That was what she'd said, or something very like it.

Wouldn't Lottie have a photograph? Wouldn't she have kept a picture of her old sweetheart? Naturally she'd have kept it, if she'd ever had one. That was *if* she'd ever had one, and it was admittedly a significant 'if'. Photographs weren't as commonplace in those days, often they were a matter of going to a studio and paying out good money. Even her aunt and uncle had seemed to have only one photograph of their only son, or only one she'd ever seen. Nevertheless it was a distinct possibility. Well worth a try.

Eileen swung her legs off the bed and stood up, suddenly feeling better for having something positive to do. The prospect of action, of something she could usefully do, always energised her. She would go and visit Lottie.

When she knocked on the door, Lottie answered. That came as a relief; it would have been a frustrating anticlimax had she been out shopping or something. But no, there she was in the doorway wearing the same floral apron and the same ready smile. "Hello. What a surprise. Lottie didn't expect to see you again - or not so soon, anyway. Come in, come in, I'll make us a pot of tea."

Eileen stepped inside. "Don't bother, please, not on my account."

"Oh, it's no bother. I'm always making tea. Lottie can't do without her tea, war or no war."

So Eileen was condemned to the sickly tea, unable to refuse without giving offence; hopefully it would be worth it.

"What brings you back so soon?" Lottie asked once the tea had been placed, as before, on the floor because there was nowhere else for it. "Are you after more old gossip? Lottie has lots of gossip, you know. She's well known for it." She giggled. "Not always popular, that depends on the gossip and who's asking for it, but definitely well known."

"No, it's not gossip exactly, not this time." Eileen ignored the tea, hoping Lottie wouldn't notice. "I was just wondering... Oh dear, this is rather a difficult subject."

"Don't you worry about it dear, just come out with it. Lottie isn't easily offended."

"Well the thing is..." Ragley's typical phrase. It must be catching, she thought irritably, like measles. "It's about the body at number thirteen."

"Of course it is. I thought it must be. Have they identified it yet?"

"No. It could be either of two people."

Lottie nodded eagerly. "Obviously. It's David or Paul, isn't it? Drink up your tea, dear, don't let it go cold."

"No." Reluctantly, Eileen sipped her tea. It hadn't improved since the last time. "Nobody knows, you see, which of them it is. I came to see whether you could help."

"I shouldn't think so, dear. I told you almost everything last time."

"Almost?" Eileen latched onto the word eagerly. "You mean there's more? Something you haven't mentioned yet? Perhaps something you'd forgotten."

"Not forgotten, no. It's just that it didn't seem very important. You see, the Berwicks always said David had been killed in the war, they told everybody that."

"Yes. They said that to me."

"He might have been, of course. A lot of men were."

"They were. It must have been a very bad time." Eileen was simply making encouraging noises to keep Lottie talking - not that she seemed to need much encouragement.

"It was. You'd be much too young to remember, but it was. Just like now. Well, not exactly the same but still bad. Bad in a different way." Lottie paused for a moment, her mind apparently drifting back to the difficult days of her youth. Then she visibly collected herself and sat up. "Where was I? Oh yes, what happened after David and Paul disappeared. You see, a couple of days later a pair of military police turned up at number thirteen. Lottie saw them. I don't know whether anybody else did, but if they did they never talked about it. They don't talk much in Botolph Street. Anyway, the military police turned up and went into the house. They came back again too, a few days later for a second visit. Now, Lottie may not be all that bright but she's not stupid either. She asked herself what they could be doing there and she could only think of one answer; they were looking for David. They wouldn't have been looking for Paul because they wouldn't have known he was there, but David lived there. It was exactly where anybody would look for him if he was missing. And if they were looking for him, that would mean he hadn't gone back to rejoin his battalion."

"You're quite right." It was a disappointment, no more than a little extra detail about something she already knew. "It's in his army records."

"So it's not news to you. You know quite a lot, don't you?"

Eileen tried to evade the question by changing the subject. "What I'd actually hoped is that you may have a photograph of David."

"Why? Surely a photograph wouldn't help identify him, not if the body's been there that long. It would be all bone by now." Lottie was sharper than she seemed.

"It's not that. It's that if he's still alive, if he actually did desert and lived, in that case it might help identify him."

94

"But then he'd get into trouble, wouldn't he? Lottie couldn't help you get him into trouble, she really couldn't. He was such a nice boy."

"It wouldn't get him into any trouble," Eileen reassured her. "Not after all these years. That's not what this is about."

"I'm not at all sure what it *is* all about," said Lottie. "Why is a WAAF sergeant so concerned with something that happened all those years ago? It's not your business, is it? I mean, I know you're a relative and all that, but... why does it matter?"

"It does. I can't explain, I'm not allowed to, but it does matter and it's not personal or family. Do you have a photograph?"

Lottie stared at her for a moment then came to a decision. "Yes, I do. You're sure he won't come to any harm if he's still alive?"

"I'm sure," Eileen affirmed, hoping it was true.

"Good. Lottie believes you. Now, let me see..." She stood up and went over to the sideboard, opening one of the drawers. "Here we are. I always keep all the pictures in the same place so I don't lose them. Lottie isn't very organised, you see. She loses things, and I wouldn't want to lose these." She took out a photograph and handed it over.

It was a copy of the one Eileen had seen on display in Botolph Street, she had a vague memory of it. This one wasn't framed, and had become tattered around the edges over the years it had spent in a drawer, but she was sure it was the same picture. It was one of those standard studio photographs, a full length study of a man in uniform; the proud son going off to fight for his country and wanting a record of it for his parents. There must have been hundreds of thousands of them, all alike. She studied the face.

Could that possibly be Copper, twenty six years earlier? Well... yes, it could be. Possibly. The picture was quite small, a quarter plate size about seven inches by five, and the face took up only a small fraction of that. It was difficult to make out anything of the features other than a general impression of a good looking but rather anonymous young man. And the scar, of course, would have changed all that. It wasn't only the physical blemish, but the tightened and shrunken skin had distorted the shape of the face. With the combination of the scar and the years... Well, it could be. You couldn't say any more than that.

"He and Paul were physically alike, you said?"

"That's right. Not quite two peas in a pod, but very similar."

That made matters worse.

"I've got one of myself as well, taken the same year," Lottie offered. "Would you like to see that?" She bustled off back to the sideboard and returned with another picture, the same size and apparently of the same vintage. She handed it over and sat down, looking smug. "There. That was Lottie in those days. You wouldn't believe it, would you?"

Eileen was too polite to say so, but no - you wouldn't. Nobody would. What she found herself staring at was a woman who looked like... well, like Bizet's Carmen or something. A gypsy, with thick black hair, wide eyes and pouting lips; a girl in her teens, fleshy and precociously busty. The contrast with the woman who sat in front of her was startling. Which only went to prove, she thought, how depressingly difficult it could be to identify people from old photographs.

"A siren, David used to call me." Lottie giggled. "Paul said something similar, but a bit more basic if you see what I mean. A bit crude, you could say. He was like that. Lottie didn't mind, though. Broad minded, Lottie was. I had that taken for David after he gave me his. They were taken at the same studio."

That was a thought. Perhaps it would be possible to have an enlargement made of David's picture, if the studio still existed. Eileen turned the photo over to look at the back, and saw a stamp with the name of the studio and an address. The studio had been in St George's Street. So not only would the studio be gone, complete with its stock of negatives, even the entire street had gone in the previous air raid.

"It won't be there now," Lottie offered helpfully. "There's nothing there now."

"No. I know. I've seen it. Tell me," she went on, "if it so happens that David is still alive and I find him, would you want to see him again?"

"No!" The response was immediate and emphatic. "Lord, no. You've seen my picture. That's how I'd like him to remember me, just like that, not as some fat and frumpy middle aged spinster with a silly apron and grey hairs showing. No, that wouldn't be right. Lottie should be just like that photo to him, always; never changing, never growing old. Some things are better left as they were, don't you agree?"

"Yes. Yes, I suppose so."

"He can't be alive anyway, can he? That must be him in the cellar in Botolph Street. It could be Paul, but it's more likely to be David. He can't be alive..." she hesitated. "But if he is and if you find him... You will tell me, won't you?"

"I'll tell you," Eileen assured her.

"Promise?"

"I promise."

Chapter XII

There was another air raid warning that night. It came, the familiar undulating wail, just after Eileen had gone to bed. She sighed and climbed reluctantly out of bed. However, even before she'd finished getting dressed an all clear sounded. False alarm. Somebody had made a mistake. It would be number eleven fighter group here, the south east. Uxbridge would be the filter and operations rooms. Ah well, we all make mistakes sometimes. Gratefully, she went back to bed, pulling the blankets over her and closing her eyes. She hoped whoever had made the mistake wouldn't be hauled over the coals for it. There but for the grace of god...

The next morning, from the breakfast room, she again saw the car waiting outside and Aircraftswoman Dowding leaning against the bonnet smoking a cigarette. She looked more presentable, though. Cap, hair, stockings, make-up... all in order. Eileen finished her breakfast quickly and went out.

"Good morning, Dowding."

"Hello, sergeant. Same journey this time?"

"Exactly the same, thank you. Didn't they tell you?"

"They never tell me anything, sergeant. Just turn up and take you wherever you want to go, those were my orders."

The car started and took the same route, along the old Dover road. The driving was as smooth as ever. After a while Dowding said, "If you'll excuse me saying so, sergeant, it's a funny place to want to go." She spoke without turning her head, without taking her attention from the road ahead. "I mean, there's nothing there, is there? I know it's none of my business but..."

"Nothing but a farm and an old gamekeeper's cottage. And you're right, it's none of your business."

"Sorry. You can't help being curious, though."

"I don't suppose you can. However, you'll have to curb your curiosity, because I'm not at liberty to tell you any more."

"Hush hush, I expect. Everything interesting always is." They swung off the main road. "My own sergeant wasn't too keen on it, I can tell you. She thinks it's taking me away from what she considers more important jobs. Driving lorries, mostly."

"All jobs are important, Dowding. If they weren't you wouldn't be ordered to do them."

"Yes, sergeant. Certainly, sergeant."

"And don't take the mickey."

"No, sergeant. I wouldn't dream of it."

It was difficult not to smile, but Eileen managed it. Dowding dropped her at the same place, where the farm track forked off from the road.

"The same arrangement, Dowding. Back in two hours."

She walked off down the path. It was as quiet and peaceful as before though, as was always the way when one followed a path that was familiar rather than new, it seemed shorter. This time, however, it wasn't quite deserted. The solitude was compromised. About halfway to the farm she saw Maggie, the big land girl, sitting perched on the top of a field gate and looking rather like Humpty Dumpty sitting on a wall, except that she was smoking a cigarette.

"Hello, Maggie."

"Good morning, sergeant. I didn't think we'd see you again. What brings you back? Taken a fancy to old scarface, have you?"

"No, but there were a few things I forgot to ask him. You're on your own today, I see. Alice not here?"

"Oh, she's here all right."

Eileen looked around. The field beyond the gate and hedge looked empty. "I can't see her."

"I should hope not. That's the idea." Maggie drew on the cigarette and added casually, "Call of nature."

"Honestly, Maggie!" It was an outraged and apparently disembodied screech from behind the hedge. "You are the absolute limit. There's no need to tell everybody."

"I'm not telling everybody," Maggie responded placidly, "I'm just telling sergeant Eileen. Besides, there's no need to get so excited. We all have to do it, you know." She grinned at Eileen. "Even sergeants, I expect."

"Even sergeants," Eileen agreed gravely.

After a few seconds Alice popped up above the level of the hedge, looking rather pink about the cheeks. "Hello. I didn't expect anybody."

"Obviously not."

"You may be out of luck with Copper, though. We heard his bike earlier, I think he may be out about his business."

"Stupid little machine," Maggie commented. "I don't know why he doesn't get a proper motorbike."

"Money, I expect," Alice rejoined. "It must be cheap to run, and there is petrol rationing, you know. Anyway, he may be out."

It was a disappointment. For some reason, that wasn't a possibility Eileen had contemplated; she should have, given the nature of his work, but she hadn't. "Never mind. I'll go ahead and check. He may have come back."

"Don't do anything I wouldn't do," Maggie called after her as she walked on. She just caught a barbed response from Alice, "That leaves her a lot of leeway, doesn't it?" They were more than ever like a music hall double act, she thought.

She passed the farm, which appeared deserted, and took the path towards Copper's dilapidated little cottage. Like the track to the farm, it seemed shorter than it had the first time, but she was still incredulous that Copper's little motorised bicycle was able to cope with the deep, iron hard ruts.

The cottage was, as predicted, deserted. Eileen wandered about the wilderness that surrounded it, a littered wilderness that had presumably once been a garden. She might as well take a look round, she thought. It would be a couple of hours before her car returned so she had to do something. The shed leaning against the side of the building was the first thing she looked at. The door was open and, sure enough, the bicycle was missing. There was a jumble of all sorts of stuff in there; boxes and tools, rags, a battered old oil can, a jerry can for petrol and... Eileen looked more closely. Leaning against the wall of the cottage behind where the bike would have been there was a rifle. She moved closer and studied it. It looked like a standard army issue rifle, exactly like many others she'd seen carried by sentries and guards. That was an odd thing to find. A shotgun, yes. A shotgun would be perfectly understandable, perfectly at home in this kind of setting. Lots of country people had shotguns, kept for rabbits and birds. But a rifle? Why should he have a rifle?

She left the shed and wandered round to the back of the cottage. Like the front, it was an unkempt mess. There was an area that must once have been a vegetable patch because it still had some vegetables growing wild in it, though they were by now outnumbered by the weeds. There was also an old cast iron pump set on flagstones that looked as if it were still in use, a bucket placed under its spout. It was probably the only source of clean water.

At the edge of the cleared area - you couldn't call it a garden any longer - the surrounding trees were as thick as in the front. There was a gap though, a narrow one. Another track, perhaps, leading more directly to the main road? It could be.

Eileen approached the house and, more from curiosity than any other reason, peered in through one of the windows. It was difficult to make out much. The interior was dark, the windows too grimy to let in much light. It looked much as one would expect, as far as she could see. It was a kitchen with a very old range, an enamel sink (no tap because there was no running water) and a central table. The table was spread not with a cloth but with newspaper, and on the newspaper not the crockery you might anticipate but what appeared to be engine parts. A repair in progress for the bike, she assumed. She eyed the back door, wondering whether it would be locked. In a rural and isolated area like this, probably not. Unless, of course, Copper kept something inside that may be compromising and that he may not want people to find - something like a radio transmitter, for example.

She ought to take a look, really, while she had the chance. It was her duty to investigate.

She hesitated, then resolutely turned away. No. There were suspicions about Copper, Ragley's suspicions, but nothing definite against him. Not enough to justify the intrusion into his privacy. A man must be presumed innocent until proven guilty, even in wartime. Besides, would any self respecting spy leave something like that around for any casual observer to spot? Surely they'd all be better trained than that.

Eileen walked back round to the front, found a convenient log and sat down to smoke a cigarette. She had the best part of two hours to wait before her car reappeared and she wasn't sure how to spend it. The cigarette was just a way to occupy the first few minutes and give her time to think.

Copper may come back, of course. That was a possibility. But if he didn't? What should she do then?

A sense of duty was beginning to reassert itself. She wasn't here just for her own interest or amusement, she was here because military intelligence, in the unlikely shape of Ragley, had asked her to be here. She was doing a job, or ought to be. Her scruples about entering the cottage began to seem like excuses made to herself for not doing something she had a duty to do. Innocent until proven guilty? This wasn't a court of law. There was a war on, for heaven's sake, and you did whatever you could to help us win it. You did what you had to do. What *she* had to do, at this moment, was to go in and search the house. It was obvious, wasn't it? She would allow herself no more excuses. She ground the cigarette out with her foot, stood up and took the first determined steps towards the front door.

At that moment she heard the bike.

It must be the bike. It was a petrol engine, and nothing else with an engine either could or would be approaching this place. It was a thin, tinny sound, the sort of sound a small engine makes when worked hard; and it was coming not from the farm but from the other side of the cottage. She remembered the other path she'd seen, the one she'd assumed led towards the main road. She turned away from the front door - not without a sense of relief - and walked round to the side of the cottage. She was in time to see Copper arrive, perched on his bike that was bouncing alarmingly over the uneven ground. He was dressed as before but with the addition of a heavy coat for protection against the wind created by riding at speed. He had no helmet, goggles, gloves, or anything like that. The bike rolled to a halt next to the shed that was its home. Copper swung himself off it and stood next to it, holding it up.

"I didn't expect to see you again." That was it. No greeting, no welcome, but no rejection either.

"There were some things I forgot to ask you last time."

"Were there? I was out."

"I can see that."

"I have to earn a living, you know. Have you been here long?"

"Not long." Eileen wondered if was speculating about what she may have been doing while he was away. "I was just sitting and smoking, waiting for you to get back."

He nodded. "Well I'm back now. I'll just put the bike away. I like to keep it under cover." He heaved the machine round and started to manoeuvre it backwards into the shed. Eileen moved a little closer and watched him.

"That's a rifle, isn't it? At the back of the shed."

"That's right." He didn't pause in what he was doing, didn't bother to look at the rifle. "That's my Lenny."

"Lenny?"

"Yes. You know, a Lee Enfield, standard issue. I had it in the last war. Good, they are. They last a long time providing you treat them properly and keep them clean, like most well-made machines." He carefully leaned the bike against the wall in its usual place. "Why are you so interested?"

"I just wondered what you wanted it for, that's all."

He shrugged and came out of the shed, closing the door behind him. "Nothing much. The occasional rabbit, things like that."

"Most people use a shotgun for that sort of thing."

"Yes. But I haven't got a shotgun and I have got a

rifle, so I use that."

"I see, And you brought it back with you after the war? I didn't think people were allowed to do that."

He grinned at her, the usual grin that was unfairly twisted by the scar. "They weren't, but I did it anyway. What would the army do with it once the war was over? They'd suddenly have millions of the things and no use for them. I thought it would be more use to me than it would to them, so I took it with me. No harm in that, was there?"

"No, I suppose not. Do you have a licence for it?"

"A licence?" He looked surprised. "No. Do I need one?"

"You do. You have done for over twenty years, that's when the legislation came in."

"Did it, now?" He sounded amused. "As a general rule, I don't take much notice of legislation. A licence, eh? God, these officials, what'll they think of next? Before you know it, I'll need a licence for my bike. It gets sillier all the time. You going to report me for not having a licence, are you?"

"No. It's none of my business."

He nodded. "True enough. He felt in his pockets and came out with a packet of Woodbine. "Smoke?"

"I've just put one out, but... yes, thank you. I will"

She took a cigarette and he struck a match and held it for her until the cigarette was alight before lighting his own. A gentleman by instinct, she thought.

"So, what brings you back? Still looking for your dead man, are you?"

"Paul Chase."

"Was that the name? I'd forgotten. But you're still looking for him?"

"Yes. Perhaps I should explain." She drew on her cigarette to give herself a few brief moments to decide what to say. "I think I told you he was supposed to have died at Ypres."

"You did."

"But then, a few days ago after the air raid, they found a body in Canterbury that seems as if it may possibly be his. It was wearing an identity bracelet, you see, with Paul Chase's details on it."

Copper smoked his own cigarette thoughtfully. "A bracelet, you say? Not identity discs?"

"No, not discs. A bracelet." She was watching him, trying to gauge his reaction, but she couldn't. The stiff scar tissue made it difficult to read the subtleties of the facial expression

"I see. And whereabouts in Canterbury was this?"

"You know Canterbury, do you?"

He shrugged. "It's not far away. I've been there a few times."

"This wasn't in a place a casual visitor would ever see. It was in a bombed house in Botolph Street. Number thirteen."

For a moment he didn't respond then suddenly, he grinned. "Number thirteen? Unlucky for some, then. How do you come to know about it? What's it to do with the air force?"

"Nothing. It's just that I lived in that house for a while. I was curious."

"You lived there?"

"Yes. It was just before the war and I wasn't there for long, but I did live there. You sound surprised to hear it."

"Do I? I didn't know this was personal for you, that's all. I thought it must be something official. When you see a uniform you always think everything's official. How did you come to be living in this house?"

"My parents died and George and Edna Berwick took me in - as a favour, you might say. Family obligations, they were my aunt and uncle; Edna was my mother's sister."

Copper didn't make any answer to that, not for a while. He tapped the ash from his cigarette and stared not at her but at the trees, apparently thinking. For once she saw his face in profile, the scar on the other side, invisible; he looked quite different. Given the passing of the years eh looked not unlike the photograph she remembered from the Berwicks' house, the one Lottie had kept a copy of.

"Your mother's sister," he said at last, tossing away the cigarette end, careless of where it landed. "That would make us cousins, I suppose." He turned his face towards her so that the scar showed again and the illusion all but vanished. "Well, as cousin to cousin, keeping it personal and in the family, as it were, shall I tell you a story?"

"I'd appreciate it if you did."

He nodded. "Right. So where to start, that's the question. I'll make it traditional, shall I? The way all stories are supposed to start." He took a deep breath. "Once upon a time, a long time ago, there were two soldiers..."

Chapter XIII

We travelled together, Paul and I. There was no reason not to. We were going in the same direction and we were mates, pals. It was 1916, just before the big push on the Somme though we didn't know about that at the time. The train was crowded at first, like they all were in those days, but people got on and off as they always do and by the time we approached Canterbury there were only the two of us in the compartment. Well, the two of us and one old codger who'd been asleep in the corner since he got on so he hardly counted. He snored, I recall that much. Other than that we didn't take any notice of him. I remember Paul saying he should probably have got off several stops ago, but he'd wake up when we got to Canterbury; he'd have to, it was the end of the line. We both laughed about that. It was a bit unfair of us, I suppose, but the man did look ridiculous slumped in the corner with his suit all rumpled and his mouth open, snoring fit to wake the dead. We just sat and smoked and chatted, passing the time.

"I'll bet you're excited about going home," I said to Paul. "After all you've said about it, I'll bet you can't wait."

"I'm not going home."

"You're not?"

"No. If I was going home I'd have got off at the last stop."

I didn't know quite what to say about that. "Where are you going, then?"

He shrugged. "I don't know. A boarding house or something, I expect. There's always somewhere to spend the night, isn't there? Wherever it is, it'll be better than a waterlogged trench."

"Yes, but..." The old man in the corner shifted his position and emitted a louder, more guttural snore than usual. We both laughed. "But why aren't you going home? You've always said you loved your home - the farm and the dogs and all."

"I did. I still do. The trouble is, last time I was on leave there was a bit of a falling out. My dad and I, we had what you might call a disagreement."

I hesitated. I didn't want to pry, but we were pals after all. "What about? You don't have to tell me if you don't want to, but..."

"That's all right. I didn't say anything before because... well, you know what it's like over there. Everybody's bored, looking out for anything that might add a bit of interest or novelty to life. I didn't want gossip, rumours, bloody stupid jokes. I couldn't have stood that. But just between us, it was to do with the dogs. Actually, it was one dog in particular.

"It had always been my favourite dog, I don't know why. He was a scruffy old mongrel and he getting on a bit and to be honest he'd never really been much use at anything around the farm - couldn't even catch a rat, though he tried hard enough. But he was friendly and lively and... I don't know. I just took to him somehow, and he took to me. We'd been together for years. He didn't like me going away and every time I came back on leave he was there, rushing up with his tail wagging twenty to the dozen. It was something I looked forward to.

"But the last time, he wasn't there. I looked around but there was no sign of him. That was so unusual, I asked my dad about it. Had the dog died, I asked him. After all, it was quite old like I said. And my dad told me no, it hadn't died, he'd put it down.

"I couldn't believe it at first, but he was quite matter of fact. He didn't seem to think there was anything I could object to. Animals on a farm had to earn their keep, he told me. If they didn't, there was no room for them. So he'd shot my old dog.

"I don't mind telling you, I just blew up. I said things I probably shouldn't, and so did he. You know what these things are like. There's an argument, you both say things you wouldn't normally say, tempers get frayed... It all gets out of proportion. Anyway, in the end he told me to get out and not come back and I told him I'd never come back, not even if he paid me.

"So there you are. That's why I'm not going home."

I thought about that for a few moments. "You still could, you know. These things are all heat of the moment stuff. You could go back and I'm sure he'd welcome you. It might be a bit awkward at first, but soon it would all be forgotten, or at least forgiven."

Paul shook his head decisively. "No. It's not what we said that matters. What matters is he killed my dog. That won't change."

"I see. Well... there's still no need to suffer in some ratty little boarding house. You could come and stay with me, there's a spare room."

"No, I couldn't do that."

"Yes you could. It's easy."

"But what about your parents? Wouldn't they object?"

"They'd put up with it. You're my mate, aren't you? They wouldn't turn you away."

"I don't know..."

"I do. You'll stay with me. Don't argue about it, I've made my mind up."

"Well if you're sure..."

"Of course I'm sure. That's what friends are for, isn't

it? We've shared a few trenches and fox holes, now we'll share a house in Botolph Street. Though to be honest with you, I don't know which is worse."

We both laughed, loudly enough to disturb the old man in the corner who twitched and stopped snoring, though he carried on sleeping. When we got to Canterbury he was still asleep, and as we got out Paul shook his shoulder. "We've arrived, old man. Best wake up before you get shunted into a siding."

It was a cheerful start. The weather wasn't bad either, which helped. Once we got outside and left the platform roof behind, there was sun and warmth. We stopped for a moment; home and freedom, no shells, no snipers, just ordinary life. You don't realise how much you miss it until you get back.

"Hello. Davy." The voice came from behind. It was Lottie. I haven't told you about Lottie but she was a friend of mine; a bit more than a friend, to be honest with you. I'd been writing to her as regularly as I could and I'd told her I was due some leave. She'd obviously been there waiting for me, and she was a welcome sight. Lottie - her name was Charlotte but everybody called her Lottie - Lottie was quite something. She wasn't all that bright and sometimes people made fun of her. Not me, though. She had a gypsy look about her, did Lottie; dark and sultry, if you know what I mean. Well developed for her age as well, if you'll pardon me saying so. She looked older than she was.

"Lottie! What a treat. Here, Paul, this is Lottie. Lottie, this is my mate Paul Chase."

"Hello, Paul."

I could see him looking her up and down and I could guess pretty well what he was thinking. He was a bit of a ladies' man, was Paul. Lottie didn't seem to mind, she must have been used to being looked at like that and I

111

have to admit she played up to it, but I didn't much care for it myself.

"Paul's coming to stay with me."

Lottie looked doubtful. "Does your mother know?"

"Not yet, but she'll soon find out. Come and walk with us." I took her arm and Paul walked round and took the other arm. I wasn't too happy about that. I didn't say anything, but I thought he was being more pushy than he should have been. Lottie walked between us, a soldier on each arm, looking pleased with herself.

"Lottie's in demand all of a sudden, isn't she?" She giggled.

"Hardly all of a sudden. You're always in demand."

"I'm sure she is," Paul put in.

"Your mum isn't going to be very taken with this, is she?"

"Probably not, but she'll have to put up with it. Here are we, risking our lives for king and country... she's hardly going to kick up much of a fuss, is she?"

"Look here, if it's going to cause trouble..." Paul started.

I interrupted him. "It's not. Mum will come round, you'll see."

"What about your dad?"

Lottie giggled again. "He'll just say 'yes dear'. That's all he ever says. That's right, isn't it, Davy?"

"That's right, yes."

And it was, too. We turned up at number thirteen and I introduced Paul and said he was going to stay for a few days. That was all there was to it. Mum looked grumpy but she could hardly turn him away - it wouldn't have been patriotic. The neighbours wouldn't have approved. So she gave in and accepted it.

"We can put him in the spare room. I wish you'd given us some notice, though. It's not exactly convenient and the bed hasn't been aired but it shouldn't be too bad."

"Never mind. It'll be better than a trench, I'm sure," Paul said cheerfully.

"I should certainly hope so. That's all right isn't it, George?"

"Yes dear."

So that was it. Paul stayed. Mum didn't like it but she put up with it. Dad didn't seem to care. He never seemed to care about much really, as long as his dinner was ready on time and nobody bothered him too much. He just wanted a quiet life, dad did. You didn't take much notice of him and he didn't want you to.

Paul's stay worked out all right, all told. We had a good leave, went out, walked around, went to the pub in the evening... it wasn't at all bad. The only fly in the ointment as far as I was concerned was Lottie. She was with us a lot of the time, especially in the evenings. I didn't mind that - of course I didn't - but Paul paid her too much attention and Lottie encouraged him. I talked to her about it, when I managed to get her alone.

"Look, Lottie, you ought to be careful with Paul. He's a good mate, but he's got this weakness for women."

"I know." She giggled. "I'd noticed."

"Yes, well... just be careful, that's all. I know it's only a bit of fun for you but Paul might take it as more than that. What's more, I don't like it."

"Don't be so boring, Davy. Lottie knows what she's doing. It's harmless, just a bit of flirting, that's all. It doesn't mean anything."

"Not to you, perhaps. Sometimes I think you're too much of an innocent, Lottie."

"Lottie? Innocent?" She laughed outright. "Don't you worry, Lottie can take care of herself and you've no need to be jealous."

"I'm not jealous."

"Yes you are. Lottie can tell. Lottie knows these things."

I couldn't say any more. There'd have been no point. Lottie thought I was being silly about it, and perhaps she was right. That's what I thought at the time, anyway. We all carried on as we were until our leave was nearly over. We were due to start back the next day. That's when it all came to a head.

We went to the pub that evening; me and Paul and Lottie. It was by way of a celebration, though why anybody should celebrate going back to the front was beyond me. Maybe it would be better to call it a sort of farewell party. Whatever you called it, we had a pretty good time. We drank - probably a bit too much - we talked, we laughed, we sang along with the piano in the bar, it was all boisterous and noisy and happy. Everything was fine.

I met a couple of old friends and was distracted by them. We all stood around the piano singing a stupid song about Nellie Dean and the old mill stream, finishing our pints and probably spilling half of them over the top of the piano. So I didn't notice Paul and Lottie leaving. I don't know how long it was before I realised they'd gone, but I dare say it was longer than I thought - it's like that after a few drinks. Once it had dawned on me, though, I put my drink down and went after them. It wasn't that I didn't trust Lottie - or didn't trust Paul, for that matter - I was just a bit worried about what the two of them might get up to on their own, without me there to keep an eye on them. They were impulsive, the pair of them, and they might do something they'd both regret later on.

I made my way back to Botolph Street - maybe a more unsteady way than it should have been, I won't deny that - but I didn't catch up with them. Perhaps they'd both gone home, I thought. They hadn't.

I don't know whether you remember the front garden of that house. It wasn't very big, just a little patch and Dad had most of it laid to lawn but there were some bushes and a couple of trees on the edge that met the pavement. Mum had liked that; it gave them a bit of privacy, she always said. It meant work for dad, of course, but he didn't object. He never objected to anything. Well, that night there were noises coming from the bushes, under one of the trees. It was dark by then so I couldn't see what was going on, but I could hear voices. It wasn't an ordinary conversation but I couldn't say it was an argument, exactly. It was just... voices, noises. I went in through the gate and walked over the lawn towards the tree.

There were people there, of course. I suppose I knew who it must be even though I couldn't really make them out in the dark.

"Paul? Is that you?"

"Mind your own business." Yes, it was Paul.

"Davy?" That was Lottie's voice. "Get him off me, will you? He's pawing me and I keep telling him to stop but he won't. Lottie doesn't like it."

"You liked it well enough earlier."

"Well I don't now, just leave me alone."

I stepped up and put a hand on Paul's shoulder. Obviously things had gone a bit too far. "Come on, Paul, leave it. You're worrying Lottie."

"I told you, it's none of your business."

"You've had a pint or two too many and besides, it is my business. Anything to do with Lottie is my business."

"Says who? Lottie didn't say that earlier did you, Lottie?"

He turned to half face me and behind him I could see Lottie's face, pale and scared, staring at me, mutely asking for help. I had to do something. I grabbed his shoulder and tried to pull him away. He turned on me.

115

"Leave us alone, damn you! It's nothing to do with you."

"It is. Come on, Paul, it's time to go to bed. Enough's enough."

He didn't say any more, he just turned round and threw a punch at me. It was a wild swing but it connected and floored me. I went down onto the ground, more astonished than hurt. On the way down I hit a spade that had been left stuck in the soil; that hurt more than the punch. I pushed myself up.

"Come on, Paul. We'll forget that. Heat of the moment, that's all it was. But don't push it, there's a good chap."

"I'm not a bloody good chap." He launched himself at me, spoiling for a fight for some reason. He just must have been really worked up. Lottie sometimes had that effect, I had to admit. I didn't want to get into a brawl, especially with a pal, so when he came for me I did the first thing I thought of. I grabbed the spade and whacked him over the head with the flat of it; not really hard, but firmly. I thought, that'll put an end to it. He'll have a hell of a headache in the morning, but serve him right. He went down without a sound, pole axed.

Lottie stared down at him with a kind of fascinated horror, hand held up to her mouth, eyes wide. "Is he all right?"

"I should think so but," I repeated out loud my previous thought, "he'll have quite a headache. Are *you* all right?".

"Me? Yes." She continued to stare down. "He's lying very still, isn't he? Are you sure he's all right?"

More to please her than anything, I crouched down and pulled at Paul's arm. He didn't react at all. Starting to get a bit worried, I felt for a pulse. There wasn't one. I tried several times, just in case I'd got the wrong place, but

116

there wasn't a pulse. Paul was dead. I'd killed him.

"No, I'm not sure." There were noises coming from the house now. I heard the front door open and light spilled out, not quite reaching me and Lottie because of the trees and bushes. "Look, Lottie, you clear off out of here. You don't want to be involved in this. Go home as fast as you can and try not to let anybody see you."

"But Davy..."

"Do as you're told, Lottie. Make yourself scarce, quick."

She turned without another word and vanished into the darkness. I stayed kneeling next to Paul, wondering what the hell to do next. I could hear somebody approaching along the path from the house. That would be dad, pushed out by mum and told to make himself useful and do something, find out what was going on. Left to himself he'd probably have sat in the living room with his newspaper and ignored the fuss until everything calmed down, but mum wouldn't have let him get away with that. There was no reaction from any of the neighbours, naturally. I wouldn't have expected any. Minding your own business was an article of faith for people in Botolph Street.

Dad came walking up, looking a bit hesitant. When he saw me, he relaxed. "Oh, it's you. What's been going on here, then?" He looked down at Paul. "What's the matter with your friend?"

"He's dead."

"Dead? Don't be daft, he can't be."

"Yes he can. He is."

"Are you sure?"

"I've seen a lot of dead men over the last couple of years, and he's as dead as any of them. I know death when I see it."

Dad looked up at me. There was a sort of desperate

117

look about him, as if he wished this wasn't happening. I wished the same. "But what happened?"

"We had an argument. I hit him with the spade."

"So you killed him?"

"Yes."

He looked down again at the body. "I don't know what your mother will say about this. She won't like it." That seemed to be his main worry, what mum would say. "What was it about, this argument?"

"What does it matter? It was about nothing. It just blew up, that's all, the way arguments do. I didn't mean to kill him, he was my pal."

There was the noise of somebody else coming along the gravel path towards us. It was somehow a fussy, bustling sort of noise. I knew who it must be.

Mum stopped next to us. "Haven't you sorted it out yet, George? I despair of you, I really do." She looked down. "Who's that?"

"It's David's chum, Paul."

"What's he doing down there? He's not drunk, is he?"

"No," I said. "He was a bit drunk but he's not drunk now. He's dead." I was getting sick of saying it, to be honest.

"Dead? He can't be."

"Yes he can. He is. I hit him with a spade and he died."

Mum stared at me in disbelief. You couldn't blame her, I suppose. "Why did you hit him?"

"Does it make any difference why? I did, that's all. Look, there's no point standing here talking about it, we have to do something."

"What?"

"I don't bloody know, call the police or something. That's what people do, isn't it, when somebody gets killed?"

"Mind your language. I'll not have language like that. And I'm not having the police round here either, this has always been a respectable house."

"What are we going to do then?"

Mum pursed her lips and frowned. It was an expression that came naturally to her. "We'll take him inside, that's what we'll do. We can't leave him lying out here for the neighbours to see as soon as it gets light. You two take hold of him and carry him into the house."

We did. He was heavy, was Paul, heavier than I would have expected. But we picked him up and between us dad and I heaved him across the garden and in through the front door. Mum shut the door behind us, still mindful of what the neighbours might see. I had hold of the feet and once we were inside I dropped them.

"Now what?"

"Pick him up again. You can't leave him here, it'll make a mess all over the carpet."

"There's carpets everywhere, we have to leave him somewhere." I was getting impatient. To tell you the truth, the strain was beginning to tell. He'd been my mate, after all. I was used to dead bodies, but it's different when it was your mate. It was even more different when you'd killed him, not some anonymous german machine gun or whizz-bang.

"The cellar," mum said decisively. "Take him down into the cellar."

"What, down all those steps? They're steep, we'd never get him down there."

"Of course you can. Don't be so soft, just get on with it."

We did. Somehow, you could never really argue with mum. She just took no notice, it was like arguing with a bulldozer. Even if I'd felt like arguing, I wouldn't have got any support. Dad wouldn't have been any use. The steps were really steep though, we nearly dropped Paul a couple of times. Once we'd got to the bottom it was a relief to lay him down; no carpet in the cellar, of course, just a flagged floor. No carpet, so no mess. Poor old Paul, that's all he was now - a source of mess.

The cellar was never used. For one thing, it was damp. And that's putting it mildly, there was mould on the walls, black mould, and even the air down there felt moist and clammy. It was lit by a single electric bulb that hung on a frayed flex from the middle of the ceiling, a harsh and bare light. Mum switched it on before we started down the steps, we'd never have managed it otherwise because the darkness was pretty well absolute. There were no windows, just plain brick walls, so the only natural light was what leaked in through the open door. In one corner there were a few old packing cases, tea chests that had been thrown out years ago and left to rot. Except for those, the place was empty and in the stark light from that bulb it looked like a prison cell - bigger than most, perhaps, but even more bleak. What a place to end up, I thought; for all his faults, Paul deserved better than that. Still, he wouldn't know anything about it and it could just as easily have been a shell hole in no man's land, or worse.

"Now what?" I said, again.

"Don't keep saying that, let me think. I'm not having the police in here, and that's final. They'd arrest you."

"I expect they would. That's their job. There's not a lot we can do about, is there? I killed him and that's all there is to it."

"No it's not. I'm not asking why you did it but I expect that tart had something to do with it. You should never have associated with her, she isn't suitable. I've told you that over and over again."

"You have that," I agreed sourly.

"But that's not the point. That's water under the

bridge, that is. What you should do now..." She paused for thought, then went on quickly. "You should go back to your unit as if nothing had happened. Just return from your leave exactly as you would have done."

"What about Paul?"

"Leave him to us. I'll take care of it."

I shook my head slowly. "No. That won't work. We fought together, we went on leave together, we got on the same train... you'd have the military police round looking for him, they'd be bound to make the connection. They're not that stupid. And once they started nosing about they'd find enough people around here who'd seen him. It's a dead loss. Besides, you can't just leave him down here."

"Why not?"

I sighed. "Look, I've had more experience of these things than you. I wish I hadn't, but I have. He'll start to smell. Quite quickly. And believe me, there's nothing quite like it. You recognise it straight away once you've known it. It's a bloody awful smell."

"Mind your language. I've told you before, I won't have language like that in this house."

"Keeping the language clean wouldn't stop him smelling. By the time the military police got here they wouldn't need to ask any questions, they'd be able to just follow their noses. Face up to it, mum; we need to call the police and tell them everything. It's the only thing we can do."

"Your trouble is you give up too easily. We can cope with having the body here. That's right isn't it, George?"

"Yes dear."

"We'll find a way round the problem." She couldn't quite bring herself to mention the smell; that would have been too crude. "We don't use the cellar anyway. We'll seal it off, brick up the door. You can do that can't you, George?"

"Yes dear." For once dad didn't sound quite convincing. Bricklaying wasn't exactly in his line.

"The smell will come up through the floorboards."

"Stop making objections. Anybody'd think you *wanted* to be accused of murder." She paused. "I've just had another idea." That was ominous. When mum had an idea, she stuck to it like glue, no matter what, however stupid it might be. "Even if they do find the body, what if it wasn't Paul Chase's?"

Even by mum's standards, that wasn't particularly bright.

"But it is."

"How would they know?"

"Mum, he's got identity tags, leave papers... all sorts of things that identify him."

"Exactly," she cried triumphantly. "That's the only way they'd know. We'll get rid of them. Even better, we'll swap them with yours."

"What?" I could hardly believe what I was hearing. "What would that achieve?"

"Don't be dense. If they think you're dead they won't come looking for you, will they? It's obvious. Sometimes I despair of you, I really do."

Obvious? Couldn't she see it? Swapping identities wouldn't achieve anything. If they thought Paul Chase was dead they'd come looking for David Berwick. If they thought David Berwick was dead, they'd come looking for Paul Chase - and that would be me. She could be unbelievably stupid, my mum. It wouldn't achieve anything at all. Except... I thought again. Maybe there was something it could achieve.

Paul wouldn't be reporting back to his unit. He'd been posted elsewhere. I remembered we'd joked about it on the train, on our way here. "Royal Engineers?" I'd jeered. "There's a soft option for you. No more trenches, no more

more mortars and whizz-bangs, you've got it made, chum. Just a spell of training that'll be useful to you in civvy street, then spend the rest of the war fiddling about with machines. I tell you, I wish I was in your shoes."

In the cellar, I stared down at Paul's body. I didn't want to be in his shoes now; they were a dead man's shoes. Nobody wants that. But if he hadn't been dead, if things were different...

There wouldn't be anybody he knew in the Engineers. The chances would be a thousand to one. If somebody who looked like him turned up with all the right identification... Well, who'd know the difference?

Did I feel guilty about it? No, I didn't. When a man's dead, he's dead. You get used to that at the front. I'd known men who'd sheltered behind the bodies of dead mates, using them as sandbags to absorb the bullets. They hadn't felt guilty, they'd just been staying alive. This wasn't much different, was it? So I didn't tell mum how stupid her idea was.

"You know, mum," I said instead, "I think you've had a good idea for once."

Chapter XIV

"And did you believe him?"

Eileen and Ragley were sitting on the bench by the Dane John, staring at the place where the bandstand used to be. Ragley had his pipe in his hand but wasn't smoking it. He'd run out of tobacco and looked rather downcast as a result.

"I think so, on the whole. I don't know about all the details. It was a long time ago, and the mind plays tricks. You think you remember things, it's not a deliberate deception, but sometimes it's possible to deceive yourself, to convince yourself that's how it was."

Ragley nodded. "Yes, I know what you mean. We all do it. But basically you think the story was true?"

"Basically, yes. The only thing I wasn't convinced by was all that stuff about hitting Chase with the spade. That didn't entirely ring true. What I mean is, surely a soldier would know about the possible effects of hitting someone on the head like that. After all, that's why they wear tin hats, isn't it? To stop things like that happening. Not with spades, of course, but with shells, shrapnel, that sort of thing."

"Yes indeed. That sort of thing." Ragley smiled placidly. Perhaps he was thinking of the time he'd had to wear a tin helmet. "I wondered about that myself, when you told me." He stared down morosely at the empty bowl of his pipe. "I'll have to get some more tobacco on my way back."

"Your way back where?"

"Pardon?"

"I don't know where you're staying," Eileen explained patiently. "Whenever I want to see you I have to either ask at the police station or come here in the hope you're eating your lunch. It's quite ridiculous. It would be useful to know where to contact you with a bit more certainty, but you've never told me where I can find you."

"Haven't I?" He looked surprised and a little guilty, like someone caught out in a social *faux-pas*. "You're right, so I haven't. That was remiss of me. But the thing is, about your cousin... It could be that his story was, as you said, basically true, but that he was trying to show himself in the best possible light, as it were. Perhaps it was all much as he said except that the business with the spade was deliberate. Perhaps he actually wanted to kill Chase and take his place."

"That's a pretty cynical suggestion."

Ragley laughed. "Oh, I'm a pretty cynical sort of chap. You get like that after a while. I'm not saying it *was* like that, mind you; just that it *might* have been. It's something to think about, isn't it?"

"I suppose so." Eileen wasn't convinced.

"The thing is," Ragley went on placidly, "he probably needn't have worried about having killed his pal, especially if he could claim it was accidental or self defence. Remember, this was 1916. In those days a serving soldier could get away with almost anything - even murder sometimes. They were heroes, risking their lives to defend their country. No jury would convict a soldier of anything, even if he was blatantly guilty. It would have been unpatriotic. He could have gone to the police without any worries."

"Except," Eileen pointed out, "that his mother wouldn't have liked it."

"True. And also that he'd still have ended up back in the trenches."

"Yes. That supports your idea of it being deliberate, doesn't it?"

"It does, to an extent. But it's all speculation anyway. Ah well... I don't suppose we'll ever know for certain. From my point of view it doesn't even matter much. What matters to me is that I'm now fairly certain who died in Botolph Street and who Copper really is. What I need to know now is how our normally reliable source in Germany named a man who'd been dead for more than twenty years as one of their agents. But that's my problem, not yours." He stood up and pushed the cold pipe into his pocket. "You've been a great help, sergeant, and I'd like to thank you. But I think you've done your bit now. You've sorted out what happened in Botolph Street and how the body came to be there. That's your part over and done with. The rest is up to me."

"Hold on a moment." Eileen stood up too. "That's rather abrupt, isn't it? I could still be of some use, you know. Copper - or David Berwick, whatever you want to call him - he's used to me, used to talking to me. He may be willing to tell me more."

Ragley looked thoughtful. "Possibly," he admitted. "That may be so. But you're under no obligation, you know."

"I know, but I'd like to help as much as I can."

"Well... If you're sure."

"I am. Besides..." She grinned at him, "I'm curious. I'd like to know what happened next."

"Like reading an Agatha Christie, you mean?"

"Something like that. If you could see your way to extending the use of the car and driver I could talk to him again tomorrow."

"Yes." He nodded absently. "Oh yes, I could certainly do that."

His hand was in his coat pocket, fiddling with the

pipe for which he had no tobacco. Eileen produced a pack of cigarettes and offered it to him. "Here, have one of these for the time being."

"What? Oh, no thank you. I don't care for them. I'll pick up some tobacco soon enough. And I'll see that the car calls for you as usual tomorrow." He paused. "It's very conscientious of you, sergeant. Beyond the call of duty, as they say."

"Nonsense. I told you, I'm curious. Besides," she grinned at him mischievously, "I've got some leave to use up, haven't I?"

"So you have. I'd quite forgotten that."

He turned and walked slowly away towards the town. Forgotten? Who did he think he was fooling? Eileen watched him go and thought to herself that he still hadn't told her where he was staying. It was quite irritating. *He* was quite irritating sometimes. On impulse, she walked after him, at some distance behind. She wanted to know where he was staying. She'd follow him, she thought, like spies (or agents) were supposed to do.

Following someone turned out to be more difficult than she'd imagined. To begin with, he was a very slow mover. It was hard to moderate her natural stride to keep pace with his casual, unhurried progress. She had to keep stopping then catching up again, otherwise she would simply have overtaken him. He never looked back, but even so she felt extremely conspicuous. It was hard to believe he wouldn't notice her presence. There were a lot of people in uniform amongst the crowds in town, but most of the uniforms seemed to be khaki or navy blue; there was little evidence of the RAF in the streets and none of the RAF uniforms she saw seemed to involve skirts. She felt she must stand out like the proverbial sore thumb.

Despite her best efforts, she kept finding herself

getting too close to Ragley's back. Frequent pauses were necessary. In novels she'd read people dealt with that by staring into shop windows or tying their shoelaces. Those ploys turned out to be most unsatisfactory. For one thing, there were large stretches of street where there were no shop windows to look into; they'd been blown out, or the shops themselves were no longer there. Even where the shops were intact she ended up looking into the windows of some quite incongruous places (including an embarrassing one which sold gentlemen's surgical appliances) and crouching down over her shoes while impatient pedestrians edged round her, no doubt privately cursing the obstruction she was causing. She rapidly abandoned that particular ploy on the grounds that she was drawing attention to herself which was precisely what she was trying so hard to avoid. Ragley, through all this, maintained his slow and plodding progress without once looking over his shoulder or appearing to notice her.

Eventually, true to his word, he stopped and entered a tobacconist. It presented Eileen with something of a dilemma. There were limits to how long one could stand and stare into shop windows. Also, when people came out of shops it was common for them to pause and look around before moving on. She'd done it herself, and it was quite likely Ragley would do it too. She took a decision and strode on quickly, crossing to the other side of the street so as not to pass the open door of the tobacconist too closely. Once safely (she hoped) past it, she turned into a side street. It was one that had suffered heavily from the bombing; there was little left but ruins. That wasn't welcome because it left her quite exposed, with no crowds to hide amongst. But she could see the entrance to the tobacconist quite clearly. She edged back behind the remains of a brick wall and watched, lighting a cigarette to keep herself calm.

128

Ragley seemed to be a long time in the shop, though that may have been her own subjective reaction. Probably he was no longer than you would expect, it just felt like that. As she stood there trying to be inconspicuous a young man walked past, saw her and hesitated. Oh no, she thought, not now of all times.

He looked like a spiv; the loose suit with wide lapels, the oiled hair and thin moustache, ostentatious rings on his fingers. Even at the best of times she would have put him off, and this wasn't the best of times. He walked over to her.

"Hello, sergeant. Like a cigarette?"

"I've already got one, hadn't you noticed?"

"No, I hadn't. Pity. They're american, these. Very good. I got them from a GI. I can get a lot more."

"I'm sure you can." There was still no sign of Ragley appearing.

"Anything else I can do for you? How about a coffee? Or a drink? I know places we could get a drink, even at this time of day."

"Do you?" He was drawing attention to her, she could feel it. She smiled at him, a bright and totally artificial smile, then leaned forward and murmured something into his ear. He took an involuntary and alarmed step backwards.

"Here, there's no need to be like that about it. I was only trying to be friendly."

"Then go and be friendly to somebody else."

"I will if that's how you feel about it. And there was no call to be so crude and insulting."

"I wasn't being insulting, I was just being honest. Now go away."

He did, just in time for Eileen to catch Ragley emerging from the shop. She dropped the cigarette and tried to shrink back into the ruined brickwork. Ragley stood outside the shop for a few moments, carefully filling and lighting his pipe. Then he strolled on in the same direction as before without looking around at all. It was almost too good to be true. Eileen fell in behind him at a discreet distance. He was now trailing a wake of occasional drifts of curiously contented looking smoke and if anything, walking even more slowly than before. Eileen followed him, trying as always to keep a good distance between them. There was, she thought, something almost odd about the way he never looked back. Most people did, every now and then, but Ragley... never.

Eventually he turned into a side road and from there into another. The shops had all gone now, it was just rows of houses, and there was hardly anyone about. Eileen dropped even further back, as far as she dared without actually losing sight of him for more than a few seconds. The street they were in was a terraced version of Botolph Street, the houses set back a little from the road and all anonymously respectable. Ragley turned into one of them, climbed the steps to the front door and let himself in. He didn't use a key, the door seemed to be unlocked. Eileen gave him a few moments, then walked past as casually as she could contrive to do it. It was a very ordinary boarding house with a hand written 'No Vacancies' sign propped up in the front window.

Why, she wondered, had he been so reluctant to tell her where he was staying? There was nothing special about it at all. Why hadn't he wanted her to know? Because she was quite sure he hadn't, he'd deliberately avoided the question. Was it just professional caution, a habit of remaining unobtainable?

If it was, she'd give him a surprise. The next time she wanted to see him, she'd just knock on the door and ask for him by name. There was some satisfaction in the prospect of doing that.

Chapter XV

"It's getting to be quite a regular routine this, isn't it, sergeant?"

"Yes. A lot of things in life are, especially if you're in the services." The car was approaching the turn off to Longmeadow farm and Dowding was driving as steadily as ever. "You're not going to ask me why again, are you?"

"No."

"Good, because the answer would be the same as before: I can't tell you."

As they went along the road, Eileen was looking out for the track that she had noticed behind Copper's cottage. She was sure it must emerge onto the road at some point, but she couldn't spot it. There was quite a lot of woodland and a number of gates that opened onto the road, but nothing that obviously led from the trees to a gate. The car rolled on and the trees receded; she had missed her chance, short of reversing and making a closer inspection. It wasn't worth doing that for what was only a matter of curiosity after all. There was a short downhill stretch, a bend, then they came to a halt in the usual place.

"Here we are again." Dowding was irrepressibly cheerful. "Shall I come back at the usual time?"

"Yes." Eileen climbed out of the car, then paused. "On second thoughts, no. I may be a little longer this time, make it three hours. It'll mean a late lunch but I'm sure we'll manage to cope with that."

"Speak for yourself, sergeant. I'm very partial to my lunch."

"So am I, as a matter of fact. but we all have to make

sacrifices..."

"...for the war effort, I know. I've heard it many times before. Ah well, three hours it is."

The car turned round and disappeared. Eileen stood for a moment at the start of the lane to Longmeadow farm. It was, she thought, uncomfortably hot today; hot and humid. The air seemed to cling to you. Looking up, she saw clouds gathering. They weren't heavy yet, but they gave the impression they may accumulate later on. The good weather they'd had all month could be about to break. She started off down the lane, brisk as ever despite the clammy heat. It was the third time now, the third time she'd come this way. Third time lucky, perhaps.

Passing the farm, she saw the land girls in the farmyard with pitchforks, loading barn manure onto a trailer hitched up to a tractor. She waved at them but carried on until she heard Maggie's voice hailing her. Maggie had a loud voice, one that was difficult to ignore. Eileen stopped and walked over to the gate.

"Hello. You two look busy today."

"I don't know why we're bothering, to be honest with you." It was Alice who answered. "The tractor's playing up, won't start. We'll load all this lot up and then it'll just sit here. Pointless, really."

"It's knackered," Maggie put in. "The tractor, that is. That's why I called you over. If you're going to see your boyfriend again, can you ask him to step over and take a look at it? He's good with machines, I'll say that for him. Mind you, so he should be. It's his job, isn't it?"

"So I'm told. What's wrong with it?"

"Haven't got the foggiest," Maggie said promptly. "Engines are a mystery to me. Manure I can cope with, but not engines. They either work or they don't, that's all I know. And this one doesn't."

"It makes the most peculiar noise when you try to

start it," Alice put in, "as if it's got indigestion or something."

"Wind," said Maggie firmly, "not indigestion, wind. That's what it sounds like. Wind, out of the exhaust pipe."

"Honestly Maggie, you can be so disgustingly vulgar sometimes."

Maggie grinned. "I'm not even trying yet. Anyway, sergeant, you tell old scarface his help would be much appreciated. If he can spare the time, that is. If you're not keeping him too busy."

"I'll tell him," Eileen promised, ignoring the sarcasm, "though we have got a few things to talk about first."

Alice looked up at the sky. "Well I wouldn't take too long about it if I were you. The weather's turning. You wouldn't want to get caught out in the rain."

"It might be better than being caught in that cottage of his," Maggie contributed. "You never know what you might catch in that hole. Rain might be wet but at least it's clean. And talking about not being clean, is that your dog?"

Eileen looked round, just in time to see a familiar looking dog darting off the lane and disappearing into the hedge. "No, it's not mine. I have seen it a couple of times before, though."

"Have you? Well I haven't, which means it's not local. I'd recognise it if it was, that's why I asked if it was yours."

"Definitely not."

"Scruffy beast, isn't it? Probably a stray. Remember to tell scarface about the tractor."

"I will."

Eileen continued on her way. It was curious about that dog but she had no explanation and it couldn't anyway be of any importance. Of more immediate concern, the air was really becoming close and damp and it was especially

133

noticeable amongst the trees. She was starting to feel clammy in the thick material of the uniform. Rain, yes, rain was coming and it may not be entirely unwelcome after the hot dry June they'd had so far, but this was beginning to feel like a proper summer storm building up.

When she reached the dilapidated old cottage there was no sign of Copper or David Berwick, whatever one wanted to call him. Probably it was wisest to stick to Copper. She looked into the lean-to and saw that the cycle was there so he couldn't be far away. Peering behind it, there was no sign of the rifle. Out after rabbits, perhaps. She wandered around for a few minutes then heard a sharp crack from somewhere in the trees; yes, a rifle shot. She wondered whether to go looking for him but decided against it. She didn't want to be wandering about in the trees while somebody was using a rifle. That would be foolhardy in the extreme. Instead she found a convenient log to sit on and lit a cigarette. He probably wouldn't be long.

He wasn't. She was hardly halfway through the cigarette when he appeared round the corner of the cottage. He was carrying no prey so had presumably been unsuccessful, but his gun - his 'lenny' - was slung over his shoulder. He betrayed no sign of surprise when he saw her, just propped the rifle up against the wall and walked over to join her.

"I thought you'd be back."

"Did you? Why?"

He lit a cigarette of his own and squatted down next to her. "Feminine curiosity. I thought you wouldn't be able to resist finding out what happened next. It's like reading a novel, isn't it? You always want to know how the story ends."

"It hasn't ended yet though, has it?"

He grinned at her, that twisted lopsided grin. "All

right, let's not say 'how it ends' let's just say 'what happened next'. That's true enough, isn't it?"

Eileen didn't answer directly. "They're having trouble with the tractor over at the farm."

Copper nodded. "They would. They don't look after it properly. Machines won't carry on working unless you look after them."

"They asked me to tell you. They'd like you to take a look at it."

He nodded again. "I'm sure they would. I might do that, when I'm ready."

They sat in silence for a while before Eileen capitulated. "You're right, of course. I *would* like to know what happened next. Are you willing to tell me?"

He drew slowly on the cigarette, not looking at her. "I don't know. I could be landing myself in trouble."

"After all this time? Surely not."

"That depends, doesn't it? It depends on what I've got to tell you and who you're going to repeat it to. I don't know. You're a cousin and you might have a personal interest, but you're wearing a uniform and that makes you official. You might feel obliged to report it to somebody else."

"Who?"

He shrugged. "I don't know. You tell me."

"I doubt it will be anything to do with the air force," Eileen evaded the question. "Who else would I report it to?"

Copper laughed. "All right, don't answer if you don't want to. It's all the same to me. Whatever you said, I'd still have to make a decision of some sort, even if it was only to decide whether I believed you or not." He took a final drag on the cigarette and crushed it out on the ground. "Here we go then, for better or for worse I've made the decision. What happened next..."

135

Chapter XVI

It all worked out even better than I'd hoped.

I'd been worried, naturally. Somebody may have recognised me, or someone who knew Paul may have known I was a fake. But they didn't. The first few months were the most worrying, partly because I wasn't used to the idea but also because the first thing I had to do as an engineer was go to the training school, and that was in Chatham; a bit close to home. Not all that close, but close enough that there might be somebody who'd known one or the other of us. I lived like a hermit while I was training, no going out to the pub, no outings into the country, nothing like that. I lived in the barracks during my time off. The others probably wondered about me, maybe thought I was a bit odd, but I had to put up with that. Anyway, it worked.

The training was good. Rushed, like everything was in those days. They had to get you up to scratch as fast as they could. It was interesting, though. I took to it like a fish to water. Machines. I discovered I liked machines. I understood them. The star of my class, I turned out to be - and it's stayed with me ever since. Do you know what it's like when you suddenly find something you're good at? Some people never find it but when you do it's... sort of exciting. Satisfying, I suppose you'd say. It might not sound like much to you, but for some reason I was good at machines. I could take them apart, put them back together, tune them, repair them, do just about anything with them. I liked them and they seemed to like me. They worked for me when they didn't for other people.

While I was training in Chatham, I settled down and stopped worrying. It seemed like I'd been fretting about nothing. Nobody questioned who I was - and after all, why should they? I had the identification, I was amongst strangers. I was Paul Chase and that was an end to it. Once the training was over we were shipped abroad, most of us to France because that was where most of the machines were. I was sent to a base near Étaples, a long way from the front line. Our job was repairing stuff that had been damaged, most of it more by misuse than enemy action. There were lorries with seized engines, motorbikes that had run dry and clogged up with sludge from the tank, that sort of thing. We just took them in, did them up and sent them out again. It was easy, much better then being shelled in some waterlogged trench. I'd been right when I told Paul he'd landed a cushy number.

It didn't last all that long, though.

After a few months, orders came through; we were going up to the line. We weren't going to wait until the vehicles were sent back to us, we were going to try to repair them on the spot. It made sense in a way, I suppose, but none of us liked it much. 'Back to the slaughterhouse', one of my mates said, and that was how it felt. Besides, how much we'd be able to do without a ready supply of spare parts none of us knew. Still, those were the orders so that's what we did. That's the army for you - and the air force too, I expect.

It felt funny going back, like reliving an old nightmare. Not that we were really in thick of it the way I used to be. We never really reached the front line, but we were close enough to hear the racket of the artillery and feel the shock when the shells landed. We could even hear the rifle fire sometimes and when there was a gas attack we had to put the masks on in a hurry. That's how close we were and it brought back memories, I can tell you, memories I could do without. Every now and then - not very often, thank God - we had to go closer to the front line trenches to rescue some wreck or other. Usually we just took one look and gave up on it but occasionally we had to get it back and work on it. It was on one of those times that everything started to go wrong.

We were in a village quite close to the front; a wreck of a place like they all were, roofs blown off, walls caving in, nowhere left that anybody could actually have lived in. Our job was a lorry, a big one with its sump fractured. That wasn't uncommon, given the state of the roads or what was left of them. Axles and sumps, those were the most common problems. Anyway, I was lying underneath this lorry trying to work out whether there was anything we could do with it, when I heard my name being called. Well, Paul's name. I'd started to think of it as mine by then, got used to it.

I pushed myself out from under the lorry and looked around. "Somebody asking for me?"

It was a sergeant. He was standing there looking down at me. "If you're private Chase, yes."

I took in the badge above the stripes; the Buffs. Here comes trouble, I thought. I knew it from the start, it was instant.

"That's me, sarge." I tried to sound cheerful. "Anything I can do for you?"

"You're Chase? Paul Chase?"

"That's me."

He frowned. "You're sure?"

"That's a funny question. Of course I'm sure. A man can't get his own name wrong, can he?" Bluff it out, I thought.

"Then I've made a mistake." He was a typical NCO, if you'll pardon me saying so: full of his own importance. No offence intended to present company. He was a big

138

brawny type with a brick red face, built for bullying - and he didn't look like a man who believed he'd made a mistake, he looked like a man who thought he was being fooled. As he was, of course. "When I was told there was a man of that name here, I decided to have a look for myself. Have you ever been in the Buffs?"

"I was, yes."

"I knew a private Chase in the Buffs, before he got a transfer. But you're not him."

"Are you sure? I don't remember you, but then I haven't got much of a memory for faces."

"I have. I never forget a name or a face. Never. You're like him, but you're not the same man." He had one of those crisp, barking voices tailor made for the parade ground. Irritating.

I shrugged. "People change, sarge. Or maybe it's just all this oil." I wiped my face, trying to spread the oil around rather than cleaning it off. "Spoiling my delicate complexion, it is. Probably makes me more difficult to recognise."

He shook his head. "No. You're not him."

"Oh well, I expect there was more than one private Chase in the Buffs. Just a bit of confusion, that's all."

He stared at me. "Yes. Confusion. Yes, it must be." He didn't believe a word of it, you could tell. He turned and walked off, turning once to look behind him and frown.

"What was that all about?" one of my mates asked afterwards.

"Nothing. Just somebody who thought he knew me from years back. He was wrong, that's all."

But he wasn't wrong. We were in that ruin of a village for a few days and they kept bringing us more wrecks to look at. I wished they'd stop so we could get out, but they didn't. There didn't seem to be any end to the

139

supply of seized engines, blown gaskets and broken axles. And all the time, every now and then, that bloody sergeant would turn up and stare at me. He knew perfectly well there was something wrong, he just knew it; and he wasn't going to give up. He never forgot a name or a face, and he was proud of it. Whatever I was doing, if I looked up I found that brick red face staring at me. I wished they'd move his unit out; or even better, move ours out. But they didn't.

Then, one day, it came to a head. He walked up to me, all stiff and rigid the way they teach you on the parade ground, and said. "You're a fake, private Chase or whatever you call yourself. I know it, and I'm going to report you. I don't know exactly what you think you're doing or why you're doing it but I know you're not who you say you are. I never forget a face. And whatever you're up to, it'll be against regulations, I'm sure of that much." With that, he turned on his heel and marched off.

Against regulations. That summed it up. All that bastard was concerned with was proving he never forgot a face, that was all it meant to him. It was going to mean a damn sight more to me if everything came out. It might mean my life. I'd been working on a motorbike when he arrived, a stupid little job. Some idiot had run it dry and the fuel pipe was clogged. They could have fixed it themselves if they'd taken the trouble, but they couldn't be bothered. Exasperated, I sat down and threw the spanner away in disgust.

"Something troubling you?" It was a mate, a man I'd known since we were in Étaples together. His name was Bernie, a friendly sort of chap who took things as they came and didn't get particularly excited about anything.

"Yes. It's that bloody NCO."

"Him? Take no notice of him, they're all like that." He looked up. "Getting a bit noisy, isn't it? If I didn't know better I'd say those shells were aimed at us."

"If they are, the German gunners need a few lessons. We're no sort of target, are we? They must be at least a mile out in their aim."

"It's been known," said Bernie calmly. "But they are, you know. They're coming this way."

I paid attention and listened. He was right. You can hear when a shell's coming towards you, it sounds different. I recognised that sound, I'd heard it before.

"Bloody hell..."

The first shell landed. It was big one, heavy artillery not some little mortar or anything like that. It had to be, otherwise it wouldn't have reached us. It hit the ground about fifty yards away and everything shook. I jumped up and looked around for somewhere to shelter. There wasn't much, nowhere with a roof or anything - not that that would have made much difference to a direct hit. There was an old stone built barn with the walls still standing up to about ten foot high. That looked as good as anywhere so I grabbed my helmet and made a break for it just as the second shell landed. The motorbike I'd been working on was thrown up into the air, so it must have been very close. I felt the blast and the earth raining down on top of me. I threw myself behind one of the stone walls and curled up, holding onto my helmet like grim death. Solid stone was about the best protection you could get, but it didn't guarantee anything. Nothing did. They carried on coming, one every few seconds, and I kept myself glued to that stone wall and hoped for the best.

Eventually, the noise and the blast started diminishing. The barrage was still going, but the shells were landing further away. I remember thinking I'd been right: it was all a cock-up, they'd got their range wrong and they were correcting it. Before long it would all be raining down on the front line, which was what they'd been intending in the first place. And they were welcome to it, as far as I was concerned.

When I thought it was safe, I poked my head round the wall to see how much damage had been done. Quite a lot, was the answer. The vehicles we'd been working on had been blown to bits, all of them. I can't say I was heartbroken over that, I was glad to see the back of them. I couldn't see anybody else, but then anybody who was left would probably be doing the same as me and keeping their heads down. Cautiously I stood up and stepped out from behind the wall. Nothing was moving. I called out, but still nothing moved. There was a thick pall of dust and smoke and a disgusting smell in the air, the familiar burnt smell of high explosives. I called out again. Again, nobody answered. There were some big holes in the ground and a lot of debris strewn about but at first I couldn't see any people, alive or not. There had to be somebody, I thought. There'd been half a dozen of us engineers plus a handful of infantry; surely I couldn't have been the only one to find a wall to hide behind.

Eventually, I came across a couple of bodies. They'd been caught in the open by the look of it, hadn't stood a chance. One of them I recognised but the other... well, the other one could have been almost anybody. He was an engineer all right; for some reason the shoulder badge had survived, so I could see that. The face had gone, though. In fact, half the head had gone. Gruesome, but I'd been used to it and I'd seen worse. I wondered who it was. It might even have been Bernie, who'd been standing next to me when the first shells hit. I leaned down to look at the identity tags.

That was when the idea came to me.

I was alive, but I was in trouble. When that sergeant reported me - and he would, the bastard, he'd meant every word of it - I was going to be in very deep trouble indeed.

And after all, I'd done it before, hadn't I?

I reached down and pulled off the tags, then replaced them with mine. When they found the body, Paul Chase would be officially dead. Nobody would be looking for him any more. That bloody sergeant could say what he liked, it wouldn't make any difference.

Of course, it wouldn't be as easy as the last time. There was no point in switching the tags, I'd just take Bernie's and dispose of them somewhere. I couldn't pretend to be him. When I'd taken Paul's the last time, I'd had an advantage - his new posting. But now, if I went back to base and pretended to be Bernie, it would be ridiculous. Lots of people knew both of us. Nobody would be fooled for a moment. No, this time I'd just have to disappear.

Sounds easy, doesn't it? Just disappear. I never really thought it through, never knew what I was letting myself in for. I was just desperate, I suppose. I wasn't properly thinking at all, I just took the tags and ran for it before anybody else could turn up and start asking questions. I wasn't Paul Chase any more and I hadn't been David Berwick for a long time. I was nobody. I didn't exist.

Chapter XVII

You'll have heard the old saying, out of the frying pan into the fire? Well, that about sums it up.

I wandered about for a while, staying off the main roads in case anybody took an interest in me, always heading away from the front line. That was more instinct than anything else, but there was some sort of sense in it. The only thing I could do was somehow try to get home and home was well away from the front line. I didn't know exactly where I was going, but at least I knew where I *didn't* want to go. The biggest danger was somebody stopping me, asking for papers and explanations. At least, I thought that was the biggest danger but before long I learned differently.

I kept going through the rest of that day. At night I lay up in a little copse and managed to get a bit of sleep. Fortunately it wasn't too cold and it didn't rain, but just thinking about that made me realise I couldn't carry on as I was, like some casual tramp in the countryside. Eventually it would get cold and it would rain, then where would I be? And I'd get hungry. I didn't have any food and I didn't know how I'd get any. I don't know whether you've ever been really hungry, painfully hungry, but I never had and I wasn't looking forward to finding out what it was like. I needed food and at some point I'd need shelter. So I set about the business of surviving.

Pretty soon, it dictated everything. All the ideas I'd had about making my way back to England, they went by the board. I didn't think about direction any more, only about staying alive. I don't think I ever got more than three or four miles from the front line and after a week or two if I had reached somewhere life was more normal, I'd have stood out like a sore thumb. I was a wreck. I'd picked up a few clothes from ruined buildings, just to cover up the uniform and make it less obvious I was a soldier. Anybody who looked like a French civilian was less likely to be stopped and questioned, and if anybody did stop me then as long as I looked the part I could always pretend I didn't understand a word they were saying. I found bits of food in abandoned farmyards, whatever I could get. I slept in woods, in barns, in shelled out houses, even in dugouts in abandoned trenches.

I'd made a gigantic mistake. I saw that within a few days. On the other hand, what else could I have done? If I'd stayed where I was and tried to bluff it out it would have meant a court martial, maybe even a firing squad. Justice in the trenches was a pretty crude affair at the best of times.

I wasn't the only one to be roaming about without leave, of course, not by a long way. I soon found that out. There were quite a few who'd decided for one reason or another that they didn't want any part of the war any more. I fell in with a bunch most of whom had been getting by much longer than I had. They'd got to know the ropes. Mostly they lived in abandoned trenches. The line moved backwards and forwards at random with every attack, so there were quite a few trenches that were unoccupied. They were useful places. There were dugouts for shelter and quite often, if they'd had to be evacuated in a hurry, there were a lot of useful things left behind; food mostly, but also equipment. All sorts of things that made life just that little bit easier for a time. It never lasted, of course. We always had to keep a lookout, make sure somebody else wasn't preparing to move in. If they were, we had to find somewhere else pretty quick. Life was unpredictable.

They were a peculiar collection of people. Most of them, like me, still wore bits of uniform but with additions they'd filched or just picked up. And the funny thing was, the uniforms were of all sorts: British khaki, French blue, even German field grey. A cosmopolitan lot, you could say. The ones I was with, there were about a dozen of them in all. People came and went, but basically there were twelve regulars including me.

Five of us were British, including one Scot from Glasgow whose accent I could hardly understand at all. There was an Australian and three Frenchmen. Then there were two Germans and a sikh from the indian army. A motley bunch who didn't have a language in common. Mostly we spoke English between ourselves because none of the British knew any other language and several of the foreigners had a bit of English. It's often like that, isn't it?

At first it was odd, waking up in the morning and finding a German soldier sleeping next to you. You got used to it, though. It didn't matter in the end, it was just a difference of uniform and language.

We didn't go out much during the day, it would have been too risky. We slept through daylight and went out at night to pick up what we could. We got by with a bit of scrounging, scavenging and thieving. Like nocturnal animals, we were, hiding out during the day and hunting at night. You got accustomed to it, the same as you get accustomed to almost anything in time. Even your eyes adjusted; the sun became too bright, hurt your eyes, but you could see quite well in the dark.

We must have looked like a right gang, more like brigands or outlaws than soldiers. And that's what we were when you come down to it, outlaws. The rules didn't apply to us. It went on for quite a while. I stayed with them because... well, safety in numbers I suppose. There were constant arguments, some of them violent, but somehow we managed to get along together. One of them, one of the Frenchmen, he was the quarrelsome type. A scrawny little runt he was, no more than five foot tall, all bone and nothing else, but he had a hell of a temper. I can't remember his name. In fact, I don't think I ever knew it. We didn't know each others names in general, it was all nicknames or at most first names. You didn't tell people your full name or tell them why you were there, and nobody asked. They didn't want to know and you didn't want them to know. That way, if anybody got picked up they couldn't tell any tales.

It was the Frenchie who gave me this scar.

One day I made some stupid joke. I can't even remember what it was but I doubt if it was anything particularly offensive. It wasn't intended to be. The Frenchman didn't have much English so maybe he misunderstood me, thought it was something worse than it actually was. I don't know. Anyway, he took umbrage and without warning he went for me with a knife.

There was an awful lot of blood. He'd cut deep.

The Indian dragged him off me. He was a big chap, that sikh, a giant of a man with a thick curly black beard. He just picked the Frenchman up, took the knife off him and tucked him under his arm, like somebody picking up a sack of potatoes. It was no effort for him at all. It's funny you know, looking back one of the few things I can remember clearly about the Indian is that nobody ever saw him without his turban. It looked a bit as if it had been used as a dishrag then wrapped back on again, but he was never without it. It must have been important to him.

Anyway, I was a mess. It hurt like hell.

One of the Germans sorted me out. He'd been a medical orderly apparently, so he knew what he was doing. The trouble was, he didn't have much to work with in the way of medical supplies and the conditions in the trench were hardly hygienic. Still, he did the best he could. I really believe he might have saved my life. I could easily have bled to death with a gash like that.

The next day the Frenchman had disappeared. I never asked about him. He just wasn't around any more, that was all.

After that life went on, such as it was. A few people came and went, but the foraging and thieving carried on as normal. The months went by and it started to get cold. That didn't matter so much because we'd found a good billet, an old German trench with deep dugouts that kept out the worst of the cold. The Germans always built the best dugouts, they seemed to have a knack for it.

Then, one day, everything went quiet.

"Can you hear the guns?" I asked the Indian. I'd grown quite friendly towards him since the day he dragged the Frenchman off me.

"No," he answered. "No guns."

"Funny, that. You can almost always hear guns."

"Not today."

He was right, there weren't any, not that day nor the next. The guns had gone quiet and they never came back. We didn't know it, we had to guess, but the war was over. The artillery had stopped, the killing had stopped. You may think it's peculiar, but at first we didn't know what to do. We felt lost. Everybody else, all the armies, they'd be going home; but we couldn't go home. We just sat there and wondered.

Eventually, after a few weeks, we decided to split up and go our own ways. Obviously we couldn't go on the way we had been. We'd been parasites, living off the leftovers of war and now there wasn't any war. Things had to change.

Personally, I had no idea which way to go. I didn't even know where I was. I could get some idea of points of the compass just by looking up, but if you don't know where you're starting from that doesn't help much. I walked, mostly by night because that was what I'd been used to. The nights were cold, though; freezing cold. After a while I started travelling by day to get whatever warmth there was from the sun. Inevitably, I got picked up.

What surprised me was that the soldiers who stopped me were German. I must have been behind the German lines without knowing it. You never could know, not for certain; the front line moved around, backwards and forwards. Where it was when the war ended I hadn't the foggiest idea. Wherever it was, it seemed like I'd ended up on the German side of it. They weren't particularly nasty about it, but they could tell from what was left of my uniform that I was British so they took me in to their headquarters.

I didn't know what they'd do with me. They couldn't make me a prisoner of war because there wasn't a war any more. They couldn't just shoot me because... well, I *hoped* they couldn't just shoot me. What I expected was that they'd get rid of me by handing me over to the British, that way I'd become somebody else's problem. And if they did that, I'd have an awful lot of difficult explaining to do.

They kept me waiting for a few hours. They were based in a big farmhouse with half the roof missing and I just sat there in what must have been the dairy at one time. There was a guard who didn't seem very interested, just stood around smoking. Eventually I was called into a room that had been turned into a sort of temporary office with a desk and chairs. Behind the desk was an officer, a little chap with a thin face, round wire rimmed spectacles and a pencil moustache; I couldn't tell the rank, I was never any good with German uniforms, but he looked quite confident and pleased with himself so he was probably the equivalent of a major, at least. The higher up

149

you get in the ranks, the more smug you get. That was the same regardless of which army you were in. I sat down opposite him without saying anything. For a time he didn't say anything either. I remember he was smoking a pipe, one of those German ones with a bent stem and a big bowl. There was a cigarette box on the desk but he didn't offer me one.

When he was ready, he started asking me questions. I told him my name was Paul Chase. I don't know why I picked on that one, but it was one I'd lived with for a while so I was used to answering to it. That was the crucial answer - everything I told him after that had to be consistent with me being Paul Chase. My unit, my history, my address in England, everything was Paul's. He wrote it all down very carefully, holding the pipe between his teeth while he was writing.

Eventually we came to what had happened after I deserted. I was a bit cautious about that, but I did tell him how I got the scar, told him it was done by a Frenchman and it had been a German soldier who'd saved my life. I laid it on a bit thick, I suppose, but he seemed to like it.

When I'd finished he put his pen down and sat back, puffing on his pipe. He looked at the cigarette box on the desk, then opened it and said, "Help yourself, Mr Chase."

To say I was surprised would be an understatement. But I certainly did help myself and very welcome it was too.

"What happens now?" I asked him, not really wanting to know the answer. I didn't think it would be anything I wanted to hear.

"Now? Well, now you have answered my questions and you are free to leave."

"What?"

He shrugged and puffed away on his pipe. "Naturally. You are not my prisoner, we are no longer at war. You were brought here as a suspicious vagrant and now you have accounted for yourself so you may leave."

I could hardly believe it. "Where will I go?"

"That is entirely up to you. I have your details and I will put them on record. That is all that interests me. I would advise you, though, to avoid being picked up again and leave German territory as soon as you can. If you don't you may have to go through all this again and it can become very tiresome for all concerned. Goodbye, Mr Chase, and I wish you the best of luck."

Chapter XVIII

"The best of luck, he said. And believe me, I needed it." Copper had been chain smoking through his narrative and there was a collection of stubbed out cigarette ends and spent matches around his feet. "I got home eventually but it took a long time and there were a few hairy moments on the way - especially crossing the channel. I got caught in a channel storm aboard a dilapidated old fishing boat. I honestly thought I was going to die that day, and the way I felt at the time I wouldn't have cared much if I did, but I got through and I ended up here. So there it is. You know it all, for what good it'll do you."

Eileen lit a cigarette of her own. "All? It was a lot but it's not quite *all*, is it?"

Copper shrugged. "I came here. Why? That's a good question. I couldn't go back to Canterbury, I'd have been recognised even with the scar and then I'd have been back at square one. I couldn't go back to my own home, so I went to Paul Chase's instead. The trouble was his family had gone by then and the farm had been sold. Even so I managed to get hold of this place for a pittance of rent - not that it's worth any more than that - and here I am still. I live, I repair farm machinery, and that's it. What more do you think there is?"

Eileen pulled on the cigarette. "For one thing," she said, "you made a point of talking about the German officer who interviewed you and the fact that he wrote everything down. I wonder why he did that?"

"I don't know. He was being thorough, the Germans are like that."

"But why did you tell me all about it?"

"Why not? It's part of the story. You wanted to hear the story, didn't you?"

"He never contacted you again? I mean, after the war."

"Him? No. I never even knew his name."

Eileen studied the trail of smoke drifting up from her cigarette. "Somebody contacted you though, didn't they? Somebody from Germany. Quite recently."

"Supposing they did, why should I tell you about it? That would be treason, that would. Fraternising with the enemy. You can be shot for something like that."

"You can be shot for all sorts of things in wartime. Sometimes you can be shot just for being in the wrong place at the wrong time. You know that better than I do. *Did* anybody contact you?"

Copper hunched forward, looking defensive. He ground out his own cigarette and immediately lit another. "Yes," he said at last, "somebody did. It wasn't that German officer though. In fact, he wasn't German at all or if he was he didn't have any accent or anything like that. He looked like a boring civil servant, and acted like it too. He turned up one day in '39. Like you, he was looking for Paul Chase, and I gave him the same answer as I gave you. My name was Copper, I'd never heard of anybody called Chase. He was persistent though, kept pestering me.

"Life was going to get difficult for me, he said, now there was a war on. And he was right. I'd got by up till then, but suddenly there were new regulations. You had to have an identification card, a ration book, and you had to register for them. Well, I hadn't registered. Of course I hadn't, how could I? I didn't exist. But all of a sudden you had to present your identity card on demand to anybody who asked and you had to have a ration book to get food or anything else. It was a bloody nightmare for me,

153

begging your pardon for the language. I was used to getting by on the fringes, so to speak, making do with what I could get, but it had started to look as if I couldn't get anything any more. Not without official documents."

Copper's cigarette was finished. He stubbed it out and took out the packet for another, but the packet was empty. He scrunched it up and threw it down. Without speaking, Eileen offered him hers.

"Thanks." He took one and lit it. "Players. I like Players. Anyway, this chap said he could solve all my problems. Identity card? He could get me one. Ration book? The same, he could get me one, could get me as many as I wanted. Nobody, he said, would be able to tell them from the real thing. And he turned out to be right, they couldn't."

"But he wanted something in return?"

"Yes, naturally he did. People always do, don't they? He wanted me to keep an eye on a few places; ports, airfields, army bases and so on. I had to produce reports for him, notes of things I'd seen. He even gave me a camera to take pictures. A good one it was, a Contax with a telephoto lens. The germans make good cameras, really well made machines. He said I was travelling around with a built-in excuse for being all over the place. I could provide information."

"Information for the enemy. He was asking you to become a spy. Didn't you think of that?"

"Of course I did, I'm not stupid. But what choice did I have? You do what you have to do to survive. It was like in the last war when I was getting by behind the lines. You'd steal because you had to steal to stay alive. Wouldn't you do the same? Wouldn't everyone? This was no different."

"But it's treason." Copper shrugged, unimpressed. Eileen persisted. "Didn't it bother you, siding with the

Nazis?"

"I wasn't siding with them. I didn't give a damn about them, begging your pardon. I didn't give a damn about any of it. I've told you, I lived alongside all sorts in the last war: British, French, German, Indian... it didn't matter. People are all much the same. Which side you're supposed to be on doesn't signify."

"But it's different this time."

"People always say that. Every war's supposed to be different but they aren't. They're all the same. People kill each other for no good reason, and that's all there is to it."

"This time there is a good reason. You know what the Nazis have done, what they're still doing, what they stand for. Doesn't that make it different?"

"Not to me it doesn't. I'm just staying alive, sergeant, the same as I did in the last war. And if there's another war in my time, I'll carry on doing it through that."

"But you're helping them."

"And they're helping me. Fair exchange, I think. Besides, when you say 'helping them', it's stretching a point. I don't know what the stuff I send to them achieves. It's meaningless, most of it. A convoy of lorries arrives at Dover. So what? That sort of thing happens every day. A couple of ships sail from Sheerness; the same. Do you know what? Sometimes nothing happens at all. I go round and about on my bike and there's absolutely nothing going on. They don't like that, they get annoyed, they think I'm slacking. So what I do is, I make something up just to show willing. I invent troop movements or ships sailing or arriving. They don't know any different, they're satisfied. So what harm do you think I'm doing my country? What help am I giving to the enemy?"

"It's the principle of the thing," Eileen protested - but it sounded a bit lame even to her own ears. "Some of the things you tell them might genuinely help them."

"I can't think what. If they want to waste their money and effort, that's their affair. As long as I get my papers and ration books, I don't care. You can't spare another cigarette, can you? I'm out."

"Of course." Eileen offered him the packet and he took one then, as an afterthought, took a second and pushed it behind his ear.

"You don't mind, do you? We're a long way from the nearest tobacconist." Then, with a sudden change of subject, "I've told you things I probably shouldn't. It's just personal, you know. I wouldn't have told anybody else. We've met before, we're family, related. None of it's supposed to be official. You're not going to pass it on to anybody else, are you? You wouldn't do that?" He was staring at her with a peculiar, intense expression.

Eileen tapped the stripes on her arm. "I'm not entirely a free agent, you know. I have a uniform and that brings responsibilities. I can't just keep quiet about somebody working for the enemy. I'll have to pass it on. I don't know what will happen..."

"I do."

"No you don't," she retorted sharply, "you just think you do. Things often aren't as simple as that. These people... the people working for military intelligence... they can be pretty subtle, pretty devious. They may not be that interested in you, or they may think they can find a use of their own for you. I don't know what will happen but I know I can't just keep quiet about it."

Copper lit the cigarette he'd taken from her. "You can't?"

"No."

There was a moment's silence. "I wish you hadn't said that. Now I've got to think what to do next. It puts me in a difficult position, that does."

"I don't see there's anything you *can* do. You've told

me now, you can't untell it. You could disappear, I suppose, go somewhere else..."

"But they might catch up with me. Besides, what would happen to my papers, my ration books? I need them. No, that would be no good, no good at all."

"So what else is there?" Eileen looked at him, waiting for an answer, but there wasn't one. Copper sat there, smoking and staring out at the trees in front of him, deliberately avoiding her eye. An unwelcome thought occurred to her. "Were you thinking you could get rid of me, put me out of the way? Stop me reporting anything? You can't seriously be thinking that." Again, there was no reply. His silence was disturbing. "It wouldn't work, you know. People know I'm here, they'd come looking for me. There's my driver, she'll turn up expecting me to be here. There are the land girls down at the farm who saw me arrive and start out for your cottage..."

"What, Laurel and Hardy?"

Despite herself, Eileen laughed. "You thought that as well, did you? They are a funny pair, aren't they? Still, the point is that if I disappeared that wouldn't be the end of it. As I said, people would come looking and once they started looking they'd be directed straight to you. You wouldn't be avoiding attention, you'd be attracting it. That's not what you want."

"No, it's not. You're right." He turned his head to face her, and his mouth twisted into the now familiar crooked smile, warped by the scar tissue. "You're safe for now, then. I'm not going to shoot you and bury you in the back garden. Did you really think I would?"

"No." Eileen tried to say it as if she believed it, as if the very idea was ridiculous. The truth was, she'd wondered if he genuinely was considering doing exactly that. She stood up. "Talking of drivers, I'd better be leaving. The car will be waiting for me."

Copper didn't stand, but looked up at the sky. Heavy grey clouds had gathered and the threatened storm looked close. "This rain's going to be heavy when it comes. Hope you don't get too wet."

"So do I. Shall I tell the girls you'll take a look at their tractor?"

"Tell them what you like. I dare say I'll get round to it at some point."

"I won't put it to them quite like that." Eileen hesitated. "You know, things may not turn out as badly as you expect. Running away may make them worse. And anyway, I have to tell someone. I don't have any choice about that."

He nodded. "Yes. I understand."

She left him still sitting in the dilapidated yard staring away from her, towards the trees. She didn't say goodbye and neither did he. The track to the farm seemed shorter than usual because she was getting used to it and familiar routes are always shorter. When she reached the farm gates, Alice and Maggie were sitting on the ground leaning back against the trailer they'd been filling and eating sandwiches. Eileen realised suddenly that she was hungry herself. Her lunch was going to be late.

"Is he coming?" Alice called out. "We can't do anything until somebody fixes this tractor."

"Personally," Maggie said. "I'm glad of the rest. He can take all day about it for all I care."

"He did say he'd come," Eileen assured them, "though he didn't say exactly when. Soon, I expect." As she spoke there was a noise from where Copper's cottage lay. "In fact, isn't that his bike starting up? He must be coming right away."

"But he never brings his bike down here," Alice objected. "I don't remember him ever doing that, it's not far enough to be worth getting it out."

"Besides," Maggie added, "that's going in the opposite direction. Listen to it." She was right. The noise of the little bike engine was receding, not getting closer. "That's typical, that is. As soon as there's work to be done old scarface heads off in the opposite direction. Oh well, not to worry. There's nothing we can do about it. You'd better be off to meet your car, sergeant, before the rain starts. You wouldn't want to get that smart uniform wet, would you?"

"It wouldn't be the first time. Still, you're right, I should be going."

She strode off along the lane. For the first few yards she could hear their voices bickering behind her.

"You shouldn't have said that about the uniform."

"Why not. It's true, isn't it?"

"It sounded sarcastic."

"I can't help how it sounded to you..."

Eileen smiled to herself and carried on walking. When she reached the road, she checked her watch: just on time, Dowding should be there within five or ten minutes. She looked up at the darkening grey clouds and wondered if she'd get away with it. Just five or ten minutes, that was all she needed.

Chapter XIX

Fifteen minutes.

The car still hadn't arrived. Dowding was uncharacteristically late. The air was becoming close, claustrophobic, damp with impending rain. When it came, Eileen thought, it was going to be a real summer storm. A downpour. There was no point in standing about waiting for it. Dowding may have been delayed; a breakdown, a puncture, an accident, anything. If she started walking in the direction the car would have been coming from, she may meet it. And if not, she would at least be getting closer to the main road where she could possibly flag down some lorry or car and get a lift. The uniform would help - people were always more likely to stop for someone in uniform. It was patriotic.

So... walk. Don't just stand there thinking about it, do it.

She strode off briskly along the lane, trying not to look at the looming clouds. She had been going for about fifteen minutes - say about a mile at her pace - when she saw the car. It had come off the road, its nose buried in a ditch and the rear wheels lifted into the air. An accident. It was at the bottom of a slope, on a slight bend in the lane; not enough, though, to account for a careful driver like Dowding losing control. Nowhere near enough. Something else must have gone wrong. Eileen hurried towards it, breaking into a run.

When she got there she saw Dowding slumped forwards over the steering wheel. She wasn't moving and there was blood on her forehead from where it had hit the windscreen. Eileen reached through the open window and, recalling what she could of her elementary first aid, checked for a pulse. It took her several tries to get the right spot, but when she did the pulse was there and felt fairly normal; Dowding was alive, at any rate. Eileen stood up again. What to do? Best not to move her, perhaps. That might do more harm than good. There could be some internal damage that would be exacerbated by movement. On the other hand, she couldn't just do nothing.

The lane was deserted. As far as Eileen could remember there had never been another vehicle on the road whenever she was travelling along it. It could be hours before anything else at all passed by. There would be no point in standing there for hours just on the off chance of some cart or tractor passing by. Dowding was completely unconscious, possibly concussed. What on earth had happened?

Eileen walked around the car, staring at it. One tyre, the off side front tyre, was completely shredded. A puncture, then. But would a simple puncture had made such a mess of the tyre? There was nothing on the road, no nails or anything like that to cause such a disaster. She looked more closely at the tyre. It was difficult to tell, the whole thing was such a mess, but the damage seemed to be to the outside of the tyre not to the tread as it would have been if the car had driven over something. Was the tyre faulty, had it just burst with no outside cause? That was possible, but unlikely. Probably she would never know - and at the moment it was irrelevant. The accident had happened and that fact was all that mattered. The question was, what to do next?

It would go against the grain to leave Dowding where she was, but on the other hand Eileen could do no good here. She didn't have the skills or the knowledge. She needed to get help and there wouldn't be any help forthcoming along the lane. She had to make her way to the main road, that was the only sensible thing to do. Resolutely, the decision made, she turned and started to walk quickly away. Then she heard something. There *was* a machine coming along the lane, against all expectations. For a moment, hope surged. Then she recognised the sound. It wasn't an approaching car or lorry, it was Copper's bike. It had to be. The noise of the little engine was unmistakeable. And it was close.

Did it matter that it was Copper? He was a capable man. He'd be able to help, surely. But for some reason...

Instinct took over and Eileen ducked into the ditch that ran along the side of the road. After all the summer weather the ditch was dry, but it was quite deep; deep enough to conceal her from anyone on the road providing she lay flat. The bike came closer then, oddly it passed by without even slowing down.

Why? Anyone finding a wreck on the road would stop to investigate, it was the obvious thing to do. You wouldn't just ignore it and carry on, would you? Unless, of course, you already knew it was there. Eileen cautiously raised her head above the level of the ditch and watched the receding figure of Copper on his bike disappearing down the road.

His rifle was slung across his back. Why would he be taking the rifle with him?

She sat back in the dry ditch and thought. She'd joked - or at least half joked - about the possibility of Copper killing her in order to keep his secrets, but as she'd pointed out to him, he couldn't do that because people had seen her arrive and a car with a driver was due to meet her.

Well, now people had seen her leave and the car was nose down in a ditch with its driver unconscious inside. She wondered how hard it would be to shoot out a tyre on a moving car. Dowding drove quite slowly, but even so the target would be small and moving. You'd need to be either a remarkably good shot or very lucky. But then... perhaps Copper *was* a very good shot. He may be. She didn't know.

He'd gone now. She climbed out of the ditch, straightened her uniform, brushed it down with her hands and started walking briskly along the road. The little episode hadn't changed anything; her priority must still be to get help for Dowding and she would only do that by reaching the main road. All this speculation about Copper may be irrational fear or it may not. The only fact was that he'd seen the wreck and hadn't stopped, hadn't even slowed down, so he clearly wasn't interested in helping. She'd have to find someone else. As she walked, she looked up at the sky: it was heavier than ever, the clouds swollen with moisture and looking ready to burst. The air was thick and clammy with the threat of a downpour. Just allow me half an hour, she mentally pleaded with the elements, just half an hour before it starts. That will be the most I'll need.

Then she heard the bike engine again.

Copper must have followed the lane to the main road then turned and come back. Why? He must be looking for her. Why else would he motor to and fro along the lane? The bike was moving slowly, she could tell that by the sound of the engine, but it would be here soon. Whether she was right or not about his intentions, she felt no inclination to stand in the open and find out. She looked around. There was still the ditch, as before, but if was searching for her he would be looking more carefully this time, making sure he didn't miss her. Beyond the ditch was a hedge and beyond that a field with a crop of ripe barley. A few yards ahead of her there was a gate. The combination of the hedge and the barley would make effective cover. She ran to the gate and clambered over, hampered by the uniform skirt that was too long and too tight. For once, she envied the land girls in their unflattering but practical breeches and boots. Nevertheless, she somehow managed to get over the gate and throw herself down into the barley behind the hedge. The sound of the bike engine grew slowly closer then passed without pausing. Eileen discovered belatedly that she'd been holding her breath for no good reason, and let it out as quietly as she could. It came as a blessed relief.

When she judged he would be out of sight, she stood up and looked around. The whole thing was becoming more and more hopeless. If Copper was going to continue his patrol for any length of time she couldn't keep jumping off the road every few minutes, hoping for a convenient gate. She'd have to leave the road and make her way across country. It wouldn't be all that difficult, she was sure. She knew roughly the direction she'd have to take and it wasn't the sort of landscape that presented any insurmountable obstacles. At least by doing that she'd always have cover of some sort close to hand, especially at this time of year when the trees were all in full leaf and the crops well grown. With luck she'd manage to get out of sight of the road entirely.

The field she was in was level at first, then sloped down towards what looked like a narrow belt of trees that ran roughly parallel to the road. That would be her best bet, down to the trees then use them to screen her movement in the direction of the main road. She started off decisively, running through the barley. She was close to the trees when she heard the bike again. She turned and looked behind her - had she left a telltale track through the crop? No, it wasn't too bad, nothing noticeable. The barley was soft and pliable, it closed behind her almost as if she hadn't been there. She carried on, speeding up.

The bike stopped. She could hear the difference in the sound of the engine. Run, get to the trees.

She risked another look over her shoulder without slowing down. She could see Copper on his bike, stationary but still sitting astride it, and he was unslinging the rifle from his back. Run faster.

She reached the trees and had just thrown herself flat when she heard the crack of the rifle and the sound of the bullet burying itself in a tree trunk only a few inches from her.

That settled two questions, then. Yes, he was trying to kill her and yes, he was a very good shot. To have missed by so little at such a range was very good marksmanship indeed. She scrambled on through the trees and undergrowth on all fours, without getting upright until she was certain she was out of sight. He wouldn't try his luck with the bike across a field, however proud he was of its suspension. She tried to calm the panic, to slow down and try to think. She was fairly safe for now providing she didn't show herself, but what should she do next? The old plans had become irrelevant, she was no longer concerned with getting to the main road, with fetching help for poor Dowding. Her only concern was with staying alive.

The plan to follow the trees wasn't as sensible any more. Copper knew where she was and with his bike he could travel faster than her and be waiting for her when the cover ran out. She wondered what was on the other side of the narrow belt of trees, whether it was worth going straight through them. There was, of course, only one way to find out. She started off in that direction but before she'd gone more than a few steps she heard the first of the foreseen drops of rain hitting the leaves above her head. They were big, heavy drops that beat their way through the foliage; only a few at first but quickly multiplying into a downpour as predicted. Within seconds, her uniform was damp. After a minute or so, it was soaked. Even under the shelter of the trees the raindrops came down like miniature hammer blows. God knows how bad it would be out in the open.

She reached the edge of the trees. Beyond them was, inevitably, another field - this time not barley but just long grass already partially flattened by the rain. It sloped gently upwards and beyond it... Beyond it, protruding above the crest of the slope, she could see the roundels and cowls of two oast houses. They would have been invisible from the road, but from here they were unmistakeable. And you didn't get oast houses in the middle of nowhere, there'd be no point. There would be other buildings, probably a farm, and where there was a farm there were people, people who would be witnesses and possibly support. People and maybe even a telephone. All she had to do was cross the field.

She took a deep breath and ran out from the shelter of the trees. The rain hit her with a physical force that made movement difficult. From somewhere there was a rumble of thunder. Water ran down her face, blurring her vision, and her uniform was sodden within moments. She kept going, struggling up the slope against the relentless pressure of the rain, the thick material of the skirt sticking to her legs and wrapping itself round them as if it were wilfully hindering every step. It was like trying to run through cold syrup. Eventually though, she reached the top of the field and looking down - she had to wipe the rain from her face to be able to see clearly - yes, there was a farmhouse with outbuildings. She almost sobbed with relief.

Looking round as best she could, she searched for telephone lines, but could see none. Nevertheless, there would be people. She ran down towards the farm, battling with the thick wet grass. The gate to the farmyard was open, listing on its hinges and presenting no obstacle. Once through it though, the scene was desolate.

The farmhouse was obviously deserted. The doors and windows were boarded up, the outbuildings derelict. She stopped and stood in the middle of the yard, temporarily defeated. It was tempting simply to cry, but she didn't; it wouldn't have achieved anything, would just have been self-indulgence. She just stared, soaked through to the skin, despairing. The place looked as though it had been abandoned for years, as dreary and desolate as she felt herself. There wasn't a living thing in sight, no chickens, no geese, none of the life you usually expect in a farmyard. Not a living thing.

Except... It wasn't quite true.

In the middle of the yard, as wet and bedraggled as she was herself, sat the dog. She thought of it now not as *a* dog but as *the* dog. It sat there in the rain, head on one side, scruffy as ever, unmoving, staring at her. She stared back blankly. Then the dog suddenly stood and trotted off towards one of the oast houses. When it reached the door, which stood ajar, it turned and sat down again, looking at her. The message was obvious: follow me. She did, not knowing what else to do.

The dog got up and ambled into the oast house with Eileen following after. Inside, at least it was dry. There was dust everywhere, stale and cold as abandoned buildings always were. There was damp too, even though the rain hadn't got in; it was the damp of neglect, caused not by the weather but by decay. The place must have been unused for years. Her heart sank at the sight. The dog had vanished.

The room she was in was quite large, with an old palette on one side, presumably for the storage of hop sacks. There was a doorway on the opposite side which, when she looked through it, led to a smaller room with a

167

furnace and a funnel directing the heat up to the floor above. She glanced around. Still no dog, and nothing to help her. She turned back into the original room. Facing her was a wooden stair giving access to the upper storey via a trap. It was very steep with open treads, something between a staircase and a ladder. For want of anything better, she decided to try it. You had to climb it as if it were a ladder, using your hands to steady you, otherwise it would have been too steep.

On the floor above, the noise of the rain beating on the roof was so loud as to drown out anything else. The roof, though, seemed watertight against all expectations. It must have been well built in the first place, a good solid structure.

All that was in the room was a large heavy hop press - much like any other agricultural press - and a bundle of old jute sacks and tools left lying in a corner. The rain, Eileen thought, surely couldn't go on with this force for much longer; summer storms were fierce but short. She walked over to the press and looked down. She could see the room below, there was a gap around the press for the residue to be caught in sacks that hung down. The mechanics were simple but practical.

On the side of the room opposite her was a doorway with a couple of steps up to it. She walked over and peered in. It must have been the drying room because it was situated over the furnace. There were widely spaced battens nailed to the floor joists, which would have been covered by cloth to hold the hops when the place was in use, but the cloth was long gone. There was nothing there to help her. She turned back. On the other side of the room, on the outer wall, was an open doorway. She crossed to it and poked her head out. There was a gantry with an attached pulley, presumably to haul up the sacks of fresh hops when they arrived. Nothing for her there, either. If she turned out to be trapped it may provide a way out but only at the risk of a broken leg or ankle. It was high above the ground. She would have to be desperate to try that.

Just as the thought of desperation passed through her mind, she heard a familiar sound. It was Copper's bike, getting closer, its whine audible above the noise of the rain. She stared out, trying to discern anything through the curtain of the downpour. Eventually yes, there it was, approaching along the path the led from the road to the farm. He would know the area, of course. He would have guessed, when he saw her disappear into the trees and took a shot at her, where she was likely to end up.

Damn!

The bike pulled up in the farmyard and the engine stopped. Copper dismounted, hauling the machine up onto its stand. He unslung the rifle from his shoulder and looked around. He didn't seem to be taking any notice at all of the rain, just accepting it as a fact of nature. Which way would he turn? Eileen withdrew slightly into the room but not so far that she couldn't see him. He turned round slowly, assessing possibilities. At first he took a few steps towards the farmhouse but then he stopped. No, that was no good. The house was boarded up. The outbuildings? A possibility. She saw him hesitate for a moment but then discount them and continue his rotation until he was facing the oast houses. The most likely possibility. She could almost read his mind. The oasts were what she had seen from the trees, they were why she had headed this way and they were the largest buildings there. That's where she would probably be. She watched him start to walk slowly in her direction. He was in no hurry, he didn't need to be. She had nowhere to go.

He could try the other oast first. She willed him to, but he didn't. It was almost as if he knew she was there,

169

though he couldn't possibly have known. As he approached the door he lifted his head, not looking but almost sniffing, as if he could smell her.

She heard him come in, heard his slow footsteps on the floor. He moved across the room, a measured tread towards the furnace room. He wouldn't know where she was, couldn't possibly know. As she told herself that, Eileen involuntarily looked down. There were wet footprints all over the place, everywhere she'd been. Not only that, but a trail of water that had dripped from her sodden uniform.

The footsteps below continued, inexorable. He'd follow the trail and end up climbing the stairs to find her. She couldn't get out. She'd already discounted the gantry and there wasn't anything else. She needed... she looked around desperately. She needed something to defend herself with. Defend herself against a man with a rifle? It was ridiculous. But perhaps not, not if she could catch him just as emerged through the trap at the top of the ladder, take him by surprise. She looked at the heap of abandoned tools in the corner and started towards them. Then she stopped abruptly.

The heavy leather soled service shoes on the bare boards would be audible even above the hammering of the rain. Quickly she bent down to untie them and take them off. Then, in her stockinged feet, she padded over to the corner. There wasn't much, nothing really heavy; but then, if there was anything really heavy she probably wouldn't be able to lift it. She needed something either sharp or solid.

Something caught her eye. It was a sort of shovel, probably intended for scooping up the green hops. She lifted it by the handle. It was quite heavy but not too heavy. The handle was solid hardwood but the base of the shovel she could see was nothing but hessian. It was no good trying to hit somebody over the head with hessian. She looked more closely and turned the shovel round so she could see its underside. The hessian was held in place by a wooden frame and the centre strut of the frame was a continuation of the hardwood handle. She held it up and tried a short swing with it. Yes, heavy but manageable. It would do. It would have to do, there was nothing else. If she could only be accurate enough with it, it may do. She carried it back to the trap and positioned herself, crouched down, on the side opposite the stairs, the side Copper wouldn't be facing if and when he came up. She laid the shovel down, keeping a grip on the handle, and waited.

The footsteps below came to a halt.

"You're here, sergeant. I know you're here." There was a short silence. "It didn't have to come to this, you know. If you'd promised me you wouldn't tell anyone, I'd have believed you. In fact, if you promised me now I'd still believe you. Will you promise, sergeant? Promise to keep it to yourself? To keep it in the family?"

Eileen said nothing. He just wanted her to speak, to give away exactly where she was. It was far too late for anything else. The silence stretched out.

"No? Well, please yourself. I'm sorry about it, but there it is. You do what you have to do to stay alive. I told you that before, didn't I?"

She heard the sharp metallic sound of the rifle bolt being pulled back then pushed forward, loading a new cartridge into the breech; then his steps heading towards the stair, following her wet trail, and starting up the treads. It was all very steady, very slow and deliberate. She tightened her grip on the handle of the shovel, holding it so hard her fingers ached. The steps continued. She hadn't noticed how many treads there were on the stair, so she couldn't count. Eventually, the tip of the rifle barrel emerged through the trap. Eileen held her breath. After the

171

rifle came Copper's head facing, as she had hoped, away from her. But as soon as his eyes were above the level of the trap he started to turn his head, to look around.

She swung the shovel. It was either now or too late. She swung it with all her strength in a one hundred and eighty degree arc that ended on Copper's head. The noise of the impact was unexpectedly loud, a sharp cracking sound. Copper didn't cry out but fell backwards down the stairs, not a tumble like on a normal staircase but a precipitous descent, hardly touching the steps but landing on the hard floor below. Eileen dropped the shovel - it would no use to her now - and peered through the trap. Copper was sprawled on his back, unmoving, the rifle lying beside him. She had to get hold of that rifle before he recovered.

As quickly as she could without falling herself, she climbed down the steps and snatched up the rifle. She'd never fired one, had really no idea how to use it, but the fact that she now held it and Copper didn't was reassuring in itself. She pointed it towards him, waiting for him to come to, but he still didn't move. There was blood on the floor around his head, fresh liquid blood. Hesitantly, Eileen stepped a little closer, trying to see whether he was still breathing. There was no sign of it, no rise and fall of the chest, no sound.

He could be dead.

A blow to the head, an uncontrolled plunge onto the rough, solid floor... he could be dead. The fall could have killed him, or she herself could have killed him, or the combination of the two.

She stepped a little closer, still pointing the rifle towards him just in case. No, he wasn't breathing, she was certain of it. And the blood was spreading in the dust beneath his head. She had to check, had to make sure despite the risk. She laid the rifle down a few feet away, making sure she was between Copper and it, then knelt down to feel for a pulse. She was tense, frightened, half expecting him to suddenly jump up and attack her. But he didn't. Feeling for the pulse was abhorrent, distasteful. It hadn't bothered her when she did it with Dowding, but somehow this was different. She had force herself to try several times to be sure she'd located the right spot, not made a mistake.

There was no mistake, and there was no pulse. She'd killed him.

She stood up to find her legs were weak and trembling. Quickly she sat down again, on the bottom step of the stair. She took out a cigarette and lit it; the hand holding the match, she noticed, was shaking but the taste and smell of the tobacco were welcome. She sat staring at Copper's body. His head was twisted to one side, making the scar invisible. You could see the man he'd once been, the man Lottie had been attracted to. It was all... the only thing she could think was, it was all a great futile pity. It wasn't a very original thought, but it was true. She looked away, staring instead down at her own feet.

There was a hole appearing in one of her stockings. On the right foot, a toenail was starting to poke through. She'd have to do something about that. And she'd have to go back up and retrieve her shoes, she wouldn't get far without them. The track to the farm, the one Copper had used on his bike, that would lead to the main road. It was bound to. If she followed it there would be traffic, she'd be able to get help for Aircraftswoman Dowding. Mustn't forget that, it was important. She crushed out the cigarette on the step and stood up.

Couldn't sit there forever. It was time to move.

Chapter XX

Eileen mounted the steps to Ragley's boarding house and rang the bell. When it was answered by a maid, she asked for him by name. After a few moments he appeared, ready dressed in coat and hat, almost as if he'd been expecting her. He stood in the doorway and looked her up and down.

"You're not your usual smart self, sergeant. Quite bedraggled, in fact."

"Yes. I got wet in the storm and I haven't got anything else to wear. I managed to more or less dry it out but it's not fit for the parade ground, I'm afraid. My Section Officer wouldn't approve."

"Probably not." He smiled one of his cherubic little innocent smiles. "Never mind. It seems to me you're in need of a stiff drink. The pubs are open now and I know a place round the corner that has a little snug where we can be quite private. Would you care to join me?"

Obviously he would know a place like that. "Thank you. Yes, I would."

They walked along the street, Eileen adapting her stride to Ragley's pace which was far slower and more relaxed.

"You didn't seem surprised to see me."

"I wasn't, except for your rather unkempt appearance. I expected you to look me up when you were ready."

"But you never told me where you were staying. Didn't you wonder how I'd found you?"

"No. You followed me the last time we were at the Dane John."

174

"You saw me? Damn! And I thought I was doing it quite well."

"You were. It's extraordinarily difficult to follow someone without being seen, especially someone who knows you. I thought you managed it very well under the circumstances."

"But obviously not well enough."

Ragley laughed. "Never mind. Practice makes perfect, you know. Here's the pub."

They turned into an unassuming little public house. Two of the windows facing the street were boarded up but otherwise it seemed to have escaped the bomb damage. Ragley clearly knew the landlord and they were ushered into a tiny enclosed room with only two tables. In the next room, the public bar, someone was playing an out of tune piano with more enthusiasm than competence.

"A half of bitter for me as usual, thank you. And I think a large brandy for the sergeant here. That's all right, isn't it?" he asked. "You look as though you're in need of something along those lines."

"It will do nicely."

They sat in silence while the landlord brought the drinks then, once the door had closed behind him, Ragley said, "Now, we won't be overheard here, especially with that racket going on next door. I'm sure you have things to tell me about your Mr Copper - or Berwick or Chase, whoever he is."

Eileen lit a cigarette and took a large sip of brandy. "Yes, I have."

Ragley started to fill his pipe and watched her expectantly.

"He's dead. I killed him."

"Oh dear. Dear me." Ragley continued filling his pipe without so much as a pause. "That must have been quite distressing for you. I'm sure you must have had a good

175

reason for it." He put the pipe in his mouth and took a match to it. "Perhaps you should tell me about it."

She did. The entire story. As she talked the pipe smoke drifted up towards the ceiling and the brandy glass gradually emptied. Ragley poked his head out of the door and ordered more drinks.

"I shouldn't have two," Eileen said, "not at this time of day."

"Never mind. It's exceptional circumstances. One doesn't kill people every day. Not in Kent anyway."

After the drinks had arrived he asked, "What about Dowding?"

It was, she thought, characteristic of him to think of that first. Other people may not have considered it so important. "She's all right. I managed to pick up a lift on the road from an RAF lorry and the driver got someone out to her. They found her wandering along the road, concussed but basically unhurt."

"Good. I'm pleased to hear it. We don't want any more people hurt than need to be, do we?"

"No. She was a good driver," she added irrelevantly, "very safe."

"It's a pity Berwick is dead. I would have preferred him alive, but nevertheless it hasn't gone too badly from my point of view."

Eileen looked at him incredulously. "Hasn't it?"

"Oh no. After all, he *was* a spy when all's said and done, so now we have one spy fewer. Also, our agent in Germany turns out to have been reliable after all. He gave us the only name he knew, which was Paul Chase's. He was passing us what he believed to be genuine information. So all told, yes, not too badly. It's odd the way it's turned out, isn't it? I mean, it all started with a body we couldn't identify, could have been either of two people. Now both of those people are dead. What's more, they died in the same way. What was the phrase in the medical report on Chase? Something about a depressed fracture of the parietal bone, wasn't it? I'll bet the report on David Berwick says exactly the same. The thing is, they both died from having been hit on the head with a spade. Well, I suppose in Berwick's case technically it wasn't a spade but a scoppet but it amounts to the same thing. That's what they're called, you know, the shovels used to pick up hops. They're scoppets."

"Are they? No, I didn't know that. How did you know?"

"Oh, I suppose I must have read it somewhere. I read quite a lot."

"Yes, I can imagine you do." The unaccustomed amount of brandy on top of the tiredness she felt was starting to go to her head. She was finding it difficult to concentrate. "Tell me, is your job always like this? I mean, being chased about the countryside by men with rifles? Digging into sordid and depressing stories you'd prefer to ignore?"

"Lord, no! Most of it's quite boring and ordinary. But talking of jobs..." He sat back in his chair, puffing gently on his pipe. "You've a few days of leave left yet. I hope you're going to make the most of them, you deserve it. Perhaps you should go up to London, see a few shows, that sort of thing."

Eileen shook her head firmly. "No. I don't feel like that at all. In fact, I've never really liked that sort of thing. I think I'll just find somewhere very quiet and secluded and sleep right through the rest of my leave."

"An excellent idea. But when you do go back..." He hesitated. "The thing is, sergeant, I'm sure you're very good at your job - in fact, I know you are because I've spoken to your officer - but you won't be doing it for much longer, you know."

"I know. I'm too old."

"Ridiculous though that sounds, yes. You'll be transferred. It may be a good transfer or it may not. One doesn't have much choice in these things, as you know. If by any chance it doesn't turn out to be a good transfer, one that suits you... I may be able to help."

"I wouldn't be at all surprised. You seem to be able to arrange most things, though I didn't know that stretched to fiddling transfers."

"I didn't mean that, exactly." He frowned down at his pipe, that had started making odd bubbling noises. "What I meant was, you may like to consider working for us."

"What, for military intelligence?" Eileen was frankly incredulous.

"Yes. I think you may be quite good at it." He took out a penknife and started scraping the pipe out, dropping the contents of the bowl into the ash tray. He didn't look at her at all. "I can't fiddle transfers, but I may be able to offer an alternative if you're willing to consider it."

"Not if it involves being shot at."

"Oh no." He laughed. "I haven't been shot at since 1918 and I was in the infantry then. No, there are all sorts of jobs in my department. There are people who never leave their desks and there are people who parachute out of aeroplanes into occupied territories. Both of those and everything in between. It can be quite interesting at times, and very useful work."

Eileen stared at him and drank the last of her brandy. "Are you offering me a job?"

"Not as such, no. I'm nowhere near important enough to do the hiring and firing. However, I can make recommendations, and I flatter myself they're often influential." He started to refill his pipe. Eileen lit a cigarette. "Bear it in mind, sergeant. If you're interested, here's a telephone number that will reach me. I won't be the one to answer, that will be whoever is manning the desk at the time, but if you mention my name they'll be able to contact me and I, in turn, will contact you. We do tend to work in a rather roundabout manner. Tiresome, but... security, you know. A nuisance, but a necessary nuisance."

Eileen started at the number - a London number. "Thank you. I'll think about it."

"Do. There may be disadvantages, of course. For example, you may have to accept a commission." He sounded awkwardly apologetic about that.

"A commission? Me, an officer?"

"Yes. We do quite like our people to be officers, it creates a good impression, lends them a little authority. I know it's an imposition, but..."

"It would mean a pay rise, wouldn't it?"

"Yes. Yes, there is that to be said for it."

"I'd quite like to be commissioned. Would I still be able to wear the uniform?"

Ragley lit his refilled pipe. "Sometimes. Possibly not all the time. That would depend on what you ended up doing."

"I quite like the uniform."

"Yes, I know. And it suits you, if you'll forgive a personal remark. Would you care for another drink?"

Eileen shook her head. "Definitely not. Two's more than enough at the moment." She stood up. "I'll be off now, Mr Ragley, to enjoy the rest of my leave. I'll keep the number you gave me. Perhaps you'll hear from me in the future."

"I hope so, sergeant. And thank you for all your help."

At that opportune moment, the piano in the public bar started playing 'We'll meet again' which, Eileen thought, one may or may not consider significant.

Chapter XXI

She walked slowly, by her standards, working off the effects of the brandy. Not only the brandy, but also the after effects of the day's events. It had all been rather a shock. She'd never killed a man before. Neither had she ever been offered a job under such bizarre circumstances. It was all a bit much to take in.

Her steps took her, without conscious volition but possibly simply from habit, to Botolph Street where she stood looking at the bombed out building that had given rise to all the trouble. An unexpected body with two identities. Both of them were now dead, and had died in much the same way, though a quarter of a century apart. As she stared, a familiar figure came bustling along the street, shopping basket over her arm. There was a kind of inevitability about it.

"Hello, sergeant. Fancy meeting you here again, I never expected it. I thought you'd be gone by now."

"Almost, but not quite." Eileen forced a false smile. "I just came back for a last look."

"There's not much to look at, is there?"

"No, not really." A thought suddenly occurred to her. "You haven't seen that dog again, have you?"

"What, the one that was there when they found the body? No, I haven't seen it since you were last here. It must have been a stray, like I said. It's gone wandering off, I expect, the way stray dogs do."

"Yes, I expect so."

"Now you're here, I was wondering... Did you ever find out anything about Davy Berwick? I'd like to know if you did."

"Yes, as a matter of fact I did. I talked to him." And killed him. No need to mention that. "He told me the entire story, what happened that night when Paul Chase was here."

"Did he? Oh well, I suppose he was glad to get it off his chest."

"Yes, I suppose so. He told me how Paul was bothering you, and he killed him."

Lottie laughed. "Is that what he said? Poor boy, he was always a bit of a romantic. I told you how nice he was, didn't I?"

"You did, yes, but... Do you mean Davy *didn't* kill Paul?"

"Oh no. Davy didn't kill him, Lottie did."

"What?"

Lottie looked around as if suspecting eavesdroppers in the empty street. "Yes, that's right. You see, Paul was making a nuisance of himself. He was a bit drunk and you know how men can get when they're drunk. It wasn't much trouble really, but he *was* being a nuisance. Then Davy turned up and pulled him off me. They started fighting. Men are so silly, aren't they? Especially when they're drunk. Anyway, it was all turning violent and Lottie thought Paul might really hurt Davy, so I decided to put a stop to it. I picked up a spade and hit Paul over the head with it. Davy told me he was dead and I should buzz off and he'd sort it all out, so I did. Men like to take charge, don't they? To think that after all these years he's still trying to protect his Lottie, the poor boy."

The poor boy indeed, thought Eileen.

"Anyway, Lottie must be going now. Things to do, as always. You won't tell anybody, will you? I mean, about Lottie hitting Paul. It wouldn't do anybody any good, all these years later."

"No, I won't tell anybody. You're right, it wouldn't do anybody any good."

She watched Lottie bustle off down the road with her shopping bag, a rather ridiculous sight now, rotund and solitary and badly dressed, no doubt a figure of fun to many of her neighbours. Yet at another time, during another war...

One act of misplaced chivalry, that's what had started the whole sorry tale. Eileen tried to imagine Ragley's reaction if she were to tell him. She could almost see his bland round face as he stared down at the smoke drifting up from his pipe, almost hear the tone of pensive regret. Not that she would tell him. There would be no point.

She really wasn't sure she wanted that job in intelligence. This sort of affair wasn't her kind of war; uniforms, parade grounds, hard work and an enemy you never saw. That was where she felt at home.

She tugged at her battered tunic, trying to straighten it into something resembling its normal smartness, then turned and strode off firmly down the street to pick up her kit.

Printed in Great Britain
by Amazon

35952491R00104